GHOST
BEYOND THE
GARDEN

GHOST BEYOND THE GARDEN

LYNN BLANKMAN

AN AVON CAMELOT BOOK

VISIT OUR WEBSITE AT
http://AvonBooks.com

GHOST BEYOND THE GARDEN is an original publication of Avon Books. This work has never before appeared in book form.

AVON BOOKS
A division of
The Hearst Corporation
1350 Avenue of the Americas
New York, New York 10019

First Avon Camelot Printing: September 1996

CAMELOT TRADEMARK REG. U.S. PAT. OFF. AND IN OTHER COUNTRIES, MARCA REGISTRADA, HECHO EN U.S.A.

Printed in the U.S.A.

OPM   10 9 8 7 6 5 4 3 2 1

For Peter

Nightmare

Falling—

The nightmare feeling hit Elly without warning. She jerked back from the window, her heart pounding.

Falling—

She grabbed onto the desk. What was wrong? She was wide awake, the sun was shining, she'd only wanted to catch a glimpse of the tree fort . . .

But the instant she'd looked out Grandma's window, she'd felt herself falling, falling, falling—

"Elly?" Grandma said. "What's the matter? Are you dizzy?" She drew Elly down onto the bed, careful of the cast on Elly's broken arm.

Elly took a deep breath. Maybe she was just dizzy. She had been released from the hospital only that morning . . .

"I'm okay," she said, but she knew she was lying.

"I think you'd better rest for a while," Grandma said. "We'll finish unpacking later."

She tightened her arm around Elly in a gentle hug,

then helped her settle back against the pillows. "How does peach cobbler for dessert sound? And a game of Scrabble after dinner with Grandpa?"

"Great," Elly said. Grandma always baked desserts; Grandpa always played Scrabble. At least here, everything would be the same.

"Good," Grandma said. "Rest as long as you like." Then she closed the door, and Elly lay back on the pillows and tried not to think.

She filled her ears with the quiet. No bells rang, no nurses bustled in with needles and medicine, no child moaned in the next bed.

She was at Grandma's house, in the familiar Eleanor Room where she always stayed. It had belonged to an Eleanor in each generation. Grandma had been an Eleanor in this room, and Mom . . .

No. She couldn't think about Mom yet, and she couldn't sleep either. She got up and wandered restlessly around the room.

She avoided the back window. Was she afraid now to look out a window? She'd never been afraid of anything. She'd always loved jumping off high diving boards and climbing trees in Grandma's ravine and hiking up enormous cliffs—

Her heart thudded. She didn't want to think about cliffs either. She slid into the desk chair, pulled down the slanted top of the desk, and looked for something to distract her.

But she opened and shut the little drawers without seeing them. It'll be okay, she told herself over and over. Everything will be okay.

One of the drawers wouldn't open, the little drawer

in the middle where Grandma usually kept stamps and paper clips. Odd. The drawer had always opened before.

But not now. Elly put back the slant top of the desk with a sigh. Both the Eleanor girl and the Eleanor desk were not quite right anymore.

Elly tried to rest, but at last she left her room and wandered out into the hall. She passed the door to her grandparents' room and the one to Grandpa's study, and then she came to Gee Gee's room.

Here was something that had changed at Grandma's house. Grandma's aunt, who had lived here with Elly's grandparents, had gone to a nursing home.

Elly drifted across the threshold. The room seemed stiff and lonely without Gee Gee's cheerful clutter. But her china angel collection still sat on the dresser top, and Elly crossed to look at them. She remembered the bedtime stories Gee Gee had made up about them for Elly when she was a little girl.

Elly sighed, wishing Gee Gee hadn't gotten so old that she had to go to a nursing home. She fingered an angel for a moment, then wandered back into the hall and to the top of the stairs. She put a foot on the top step and—

Falling—

Elly grabbed the bannister, her heart pounding. Again, that terrifying feeling of falling. What was wrong with her? First the window, now the stairs. Was she afraid of a flight of stairs?

She forced herself to breathe deeply several times. It's all right, she told herself. Everything's all right. I'm just a little shaky.

Slowly, keeping a tight hold on the bannister and

3

looking straight ahead, she made her way down the stairs. There. She was fine. Everything would be fine.

In the kitchen, the table under the windows was set for dinner. Peach cobbler filled the room with its sweet smell, and Elly could see Grandma crossing the grass with an armload of deep red flowers.

Her spirits rose a little. Grandma's gardening was something that hadn't changed. All around the yard were flowers—all kinds of flowers, red, blue, pink, purple.

"Aren't these peonies lovely?" Grandma plunked them into a thick white pitcher and set it on the kitchen table. "This is the first year this batch has bloomed."

Then Grandpa came in. "Elly!" He set down his briefcase and gave Elly a careful hug. "How's my favorite Eleanor?" He winked at her. It was one of their special jokes.

"And what about me?" Grandma said. She pretended to be indignant, and they all laughed together.

Dinner was relaxing. Grandma had made fried chicken, which Elly could eat with only one hand, and the peach cobbler tasted as sweet as it smelled.

After dinner they moved into the den, and Elly set up the Scrabble board in its usual place on the ottoman. Grandma fussed with the coffee cups. Grandpa settled into his chair. If it hadn't been for her bruises and her cast, Elly could have believed she was on an ordinary visit.

Maybe she could pretend that everything really was the same, that she'd broken her arm riding her bike or something, that Mom was fine . . .

Then the phone rang. Dad was calling from the hospital in Maine, and Elly knew there could be no pretending.

4

"How's my girl?" Dad said.

"Okay. How's Mom?"

"She's okay too."

But Elly couldn't forget her last view of Mom in the hospital that morning—the bruises, the casts, the bandages . . . "When can she come home?"

Dad was silent for a moment. "It's too soon to say, Elly. We have to be patient." Then, in a mock stern tone, he added, "Now go beat Grandpa at Scrabble."

But more calls from other relatives interrupted the game. Grandma Morrison called, then some aunts and uncles, and then Elly's favorite cousin Kate was on the phone.

"Elly! Are you okay? Can you still work on our tree fort when I come?" Kate was eleven, the same age as Elly, and every summer they spent a week together at Grandma's house. Last year they had built a fort in an old maple tree in the ravine.

Elly swallowed, remembering her glance from the upstairs window. "When are you coming?"

"The second week of August. First I have my diving clinic and then soccer camp and then I'm going camping with Jessica . . ."

The second week of August was a long time away, Elly thought with relief as Kate rambled on about her summer plans. She would be better by then.

At last the phone stopped ringing, but Elly made it through only one game of Scrabble before she was ready to go to bed.

Grandma helped her get the cast through the sleeve of her nightgown and squirt toothpaste onto her toothbrush.

"Sweet dreams, Elly," Grandma said as she turned out the light.

5

"Thanks, Grandma." Elly closed her eyes. She had her own pillow from home, Grandma's cat Lucky was curled up on the quilt at her feet, and the house was quiet. She heard Grandma close the door, and within minutes she sank into sleep.

But then Mom was slipping on the rocks, and Elly was watching, horrified, and Mom was falling and falling, tumbling down the jagged rocks, and all Elly could do was scream over and over, "Mom! Mom! Mom!" and then she was falling herself, falling—

"Elly!" Grandma's hand was on her shoulder. "Elly!"

Grandma. Elly took a shuddering breath. She was in Grandma's house, but the nightmare had followed her.

"Just a bad dream," Grandma murmured. She brushed the hair back from Elly's forehead with a cool hand. "Everything's all right."

Elly struggled to calm her breathing. Everything wasn't all right. Nothing had been right since the moment on the annual camping trip—the one she and her mother and Mom's teacher friends always took the weekend school was out, when Mom, standing at the edge of the cliffs in Maine, had flung out her arms and cried, "Isn't it splendid!"—and slipped.

And Elly had stood frozen, watching her fall, doing nothing until Mom lay motionless and silent on the jagged rocks. Only then had she reached for her, scrambling down the rocks, screaming—but it was too late, and then Elly had fallen, too—

No. Everything was not all right.

Grandma clicked on the small desk lamp, and a soft glow filled the room.

"We'll leave the lamp on tonight," she said, and tucked the blanket tight around Elly.

She lay still after Grandma left, her eyes wide, trying to think of something besides rocks and falling and Mom.

Her gaze moved slowly around the room. The door, the window—No. Not the window.

The desk. The Eleanor desk with the little drawer that wouldn't open . . .

She sat up. Slowly she slid out of bed. She would get that drawer to open.

2

A Locket

Just as before, the little desk drawer would open only a crack. Elly rummaged quietly through the other drawers, looking for something to use as a lever. She tried a ruler, but it was plastic and it bent with the pressure. A nail file was too thin.

Maybe Grandma's letter opener would work. Elly slipped it into the small space and pulled hard, toward herself. The drawer shuddered and opened a little farther.

Now she could get her fingers inside it. She grabbed the edge of the drawer and yanked. It was coming . . . She braced herself and pulled with all her strength, and the empty drawer fell out, sending her stumbling backward.

Pain shot up her broken arm, and she cried out. Had anyone heard? She held her breath and listened, but the house was silent. Only the cat made rustling noises as he settled himself in a new spot on the bed.

She waited a moment for the pain to ease, then saw,

in the drawer's resting space, something wedged against the back of the desk. Crumpled stamps. That was what had caused the drawer to stick.

But something was mixed up with the stamps, a blackish chain. No. Her fingers tingled as she pulled it from the wrinkled stamps. It was a necklace with a small tarnished heart dangling from the chain.

"A locket!" she whispered. She pried the heart open, but the tiny places for pictures were empty.

She tiptoed to the little mirror over the dresser and held the locket to her neck. Was it silver? Tomorrow she would try to polish off the black parts.

She climbed back into bed and moved her thumb over the tiny heart. Had the locket belonged to Mom when she was a girl? Or Grandma? Elly would ask first thing in the morning.

The nightmare did not return that night. In the morning, Elly averted her gaze from the window as she pulled up the shade, then struggled into some clothes as quickly as she could. She picked up the locket and padded barefoot out of her room.

Downstairs in the front hall, she could hear voices in the kitchen.

". . . get counseling if this keeps up," Grandma was saying in a worried tone.

"Give her time, El," Grandpa said. "It's been only a few days since the accident."

Were they talking about Mom? Elly wondered as she went into the kitchen. Or her?

"Good morning!" Grandma said cheerfully.

"Good morning." Elly held out the locket. "Look what I found."

"Oh, my," Grandma said.

"Where did you find that?" Grandpa asked.

Elly took them upstairs and showed them where she had found the locket in the Eleanor desk.

Grandpa moved the drawer back and forth in its spot as if to make sure there was nothing in its way now. "The only thing I can think of," he said, "is that when we moved all the furniture out of this room—"

"We were going to paint just before the accident," Grandma put in.

"And then we had to move everything back in a hurry," Grandpa went on. "The stamps must have gotten wedged in that drawer in all the moving back and forth."

"But what about the locket?" Elly asked.

Grandpa shook his head. "It must have been stuck behind that drawer all along."

"But how could that be? You've always had the Eleanor desk, haven't you, Grandma?" Elly followed her grandparents back down the stairs to the kitchen.

"Well, ever since I can remember," Grandma said, setting a place for Elly at the table. "But I don't know where the desk came from originally. Or even how old it is."

"Would Gee Gee know?" Elly asked.

Grandma hesitated. "I don't know, honey. She gets muddled about things now."

"Can we go ask her?"

Grandma and Grandpa exchanged looks. "Let's wait a day or so," Grandpa said.

Grandma nodded. "Besides," she said, "we've got to make a pie this morning!"

Elly smiled. They always made pies on her first morning at Grandma's house. "Okay. And when we're done, I'll polish the locket."

But when it was time to make the pie, after Grandpa had left for his office and the breakfast dishes were done, there wasn't much Elly could do. She couldn't slice peaches with one hand. She couldn't roll pie crust either. Even greasing the pie tin was hard.

Elly tried not to mind, and while Grandma made the pie, she polished the locket. It was a struggle with only one good arm, but she smoothed the silver paste over the heart and then over every link of the chain.

It *was* silver. When she was done, the necklace gleamed. "Look, Grandma!"

Grandma turned from the sink where she was washing the baking dishes. "It's beautiful, Elly." She helped Elly wash off the polish, and then she found a soft cloth for Elly to wipe it dry.

"Oh, Grandma," Elly breathed. "Can I wear it?"

Grandma smiled. "Of course."

But Elly's arm hurt when she reached behind her neck to fasten the locket, and Grandma had to help.

"Uh oh," Grandma said. "The clasp is bent. We'll have to get it fixed before you can wear it, honey."

"Oh, no." Elly had really wanted to wear the locket. Disappointed, she peered at the clasp.

"It *is* too bad," Grandma said, "but you wouldn't want to lose it, would you?" She put the necklace into Elly's hand. "Find a safe place for it, and one of these days we'll take it to a jeweler's. All right?"

"All right." But Elly thought the clasp looked fine.

Grandma put an arm around her. "Maybe we can find photographs of your mom and dad that will fit inside the little heart."

11

Elly brightened. "That's a great idea." She'd always wanted a locket, especially one with spots for photographs.

Grandma hugged her. "We'll do that later," she said. "But now . . ." She slid the pie into the oven and turned to Elly. "We can reward ourselves with some weeding!"

Elly laughed. "No one but you would think weeding was a reward."

Grandma laughed too, but she said, "Gee Gee was just the same. Why, between the two of us, we've spent . . ." Grandma gazed out the back door towards her flowers. "We've spent nearly seventy years on this garden!" She turned back to Elly with a surprised expression. "I never added it up before."

Elly tried to imagine Grandma as a little girl, growing up in this house and helping her aunt in the garden. How strange to have always lived in the same house.

"I don't know what I'd do without a place to dig." Grandma took off her apron and hung it on a hook. "Do you want to come outside with me?"

The garden was bright with sunshine and flowers. Elly rubbed her thumb over the little heart of her necklace. The nightmare seemed a long time ago. "Sure," she said.

"Good," Grandma said. "Maybe you've inherited the gardening genes. Why don't you put away the locket while I get my tools from the garage, and I'll meet you in the garden."

Elly turned to take the locket upstairs to her room as the screen door banged behind Grandma. She hesitated, wanting to keep the locket with her. She rubbed her thumb again across the little heart. The silver felt smooth and warm and comforting in her hand.

The kitchen clock ticked. Outside, birds called to one another in the garden.

Elly slipped the necklace into the pocket of her shorts. It would be safe there. She turned and followed Grandma outside.

The garden was empty. Grandma was still in the garage gathering her tools. Elly crossed the grass to the old stone bench back by the honeysuckle bushes and sat down to wait.

But she couldn't resist looking at the locket again. She pulled it from her pocket. The clasp looked fine to her. It fastened easily in her hands. It seemed very secure . . .

Maybe she could fasten it herself around her neck, if she did it in front and then slid it around to the back. She reached up her arms. There. Like that.

Without warning, her head swam with dizziness, and the garden whirled around her. She grabbed onto the edge of the bench, certain she would fall off.

Then, just as quickly, the dizziness passed, and she sat, shaken but fine, on the bench.

She groaned aloud. She hated being dizzy. She hated having a broken arm. She hated having nightmares. When would she be herself again?

She looked toward the garage. What was taking Grandma so long? Gardening would be a good distraction.

Leaves rustled at the back of the garden. Elly turned and saw a girl coming out of the honeysuckle bushes at the edge of the ravine.

Elly stared at her. The one thing she had never liked

about visiting Grandma was that, except when her cousin Kate came, there were no kids around. Only older people owned the big houses in Grandma's neighborhood.

But here was a girl Elly's own size. She had beautiful hair, thick and long, and she was wearing a dress and black tights.

"Hello," the girl said. "What are you doing here?"

3

The Ravine

Elly stared at the girl. What was *she* doing here, in Grandma's backyard? She must have come from the ravine. But who was she? Had she just moved into the neighborhood?

Before Elly could ask, the girl spoke. "Are you the new people in the Lunds' house?" Her voice was hopeful.

Elly shook her head. "I'm visiting my grandparents. Where do you—?" She broke off at the look of disappointment on the girl's face. "What's the matter?"

The girl shrugged. "Nothing."

She was pretty and her hair was beautiful, but there was something odd about her. She seemed sad.

"Maybe you could come over sometime," Elly said. "I'm going to be here all summer."

The girl's face brightened. "Oh that's wonderful. There's no one to play with. My best . . ." She hesitated, and that look of sadness swept again across her face. "My sister's too old, and my brothers play tricks on me, and my friend's in quarantine."

"Quarantine?" No one Elly knew had ever been quarantined.

The girl nodded. "Scarlet fever."

Elly's cousin, Robbie, had had scarlet fever at Easter, but he hadn't been quarantined for it. She didn't think he'd missed more than a few days of school.

"Is your arm broken?" the girl asked, pointing to Elly's cast. "Do you think you could swing?"

"I don't know," Elly said. "What kind of swing is it?"

The girl leaned forward as if to tell a secret. "Let me show you. My brothers are gone right now, so we can have it all to ourselves." She glanced at Elly's shorts. "Those will be good for swinging. Are they your brother's?"

That was a weird thing to say. "No, they're mine." Elly eyed the girl. Maybe she didn't want to play with her after all.

But the girl put a finger to her lips and motioned Elly back to the bushes. "Come on," she whispered.

Was the swing in the ravine? Elly hesitated. Grandma still hadn't come out of the garage, but ... Elly swallowed, picturing the small stream at the bottom of the ravine, the rocks, the sloping ground ...

"Come on!" the girl repeated.

Elly took a deep breath. Pushing away her fears, she followed the girl back through the bushes on the familiar path to the ravine. "What's your name?" she whispered.

"Winnie," the girl said over her shoulder. "What's yours?"

"Elly."

Then Winnie reached for her hand, honeysuckle

16

branches scratched at their legs, and they were in the ravine.

It was like another world, dark and quiet, after the bright garden. Trees towered above them, cutting out the morning sunshine. On the other side of the ravine Elly could see little paths, mossy rocks, and here and there small clumps of green plants and wildflowers.

The path at the top of the ravine was broad and flat, but even so Elly's stomach fluttered. She couldn't look down.

But what she did see ... She frowned, puzzled. Somehow the place seemed different. Was she dizzy again?

"Look." Winnie pointed to a huge tree arching over the ravine. A thick rope hung from a branch stretching high across the stream.

"Ohhh," Elly breathed.

"Watch." Winnie grabbed the huge knotted end. She ran backward with it until the rope was taut, jumped for a spot higher on the rope, and swung out over the ravine, over the stream, over the rocks.

Elly froze.

Falling—

"Watch, Elly!" Winnie twisted on the rope and waved.

Winnie could slip. She could fall. The *rocks*—

Mom—

The rope jerked.

Falling—

Elly stumbled backward.

"Elly!" Winnie called behind her. "Where are you going? Don't you want to swing?"

"NO! I—NO!" Elly whirled and pushed her way through the bushes.

"Grandma!" she cried as she came out onto the lawn. "Grandma!" But no one was there.

At the back steps, she stumbled, dizzy again, and then at last she was safe, panting, in the house.

"Grandma!" she called again. But there was no answer.

She sank into a chair, everything aching, trying to calm her breathing. It's okay, she told herself over and over. Everything's okay.

But it wasn't. She put her face in her hand. She'd ruined her only chance to have a friend this summer because she'd become a baby about heights. What was wrong with her?

At last, she got up and wandered in misery to the back door. She could see Grandma now, weeding, but there was no sign of Winnie.

Elly groaned and leaned against the door frame. What must Winnie think of her? Not only was she afraid to swing on the rope, she wouldn't even watch!

Elly reached for the locket, to rub the little heart—It was gone! Oh, no! She'd lost the locket, on top of everything else.

She rested her face against the screen and closed her eyes. Everything seemed lost these days.

After a while, she made her way back outside and across the grass, searching for the locket and hoping to find Winnie again. She edged through the bushes until she stood on the broad path. She peered cautiously into the ravine. But there was no locket, and Winnie was gone.

The tree fort was there, the one she and Kate had

built last summer, and her favorite climbing tree and the big rock at the side of the path. But Winnie was gone, and so was the locket. And Winnie must have hidden the tree swing somewhere, because Elly couldn't find that, either.

"Elly, you're as white as a sheet," Grandma said when Elly sank down beside her on the grass. "Are you all right?"

Elly couldn't bear to tell Grandma she'd lost the locket. "I'm fine," she said, but Grandma packed her gardening things into a basket.

"Come along. I'll fix you some lunch, and then it's time for a rest."

Elly trailed after Grandma back across the grass. Taking naps like a baby! She stifled a sigh and put her foot on the bottom step.

Something sparkled at her from the grass next to the step, and she bent to investigate. A small silver heart lay gleaming at her fingertips. The locket! Elly scooped it up and peered at the clasp. It was unmistakably crooked now. Grandma had been right.

But at least Elly had the locket back. Thankfully, she slipped it into the pocket of her shorts.

Grandma had put her gardening basket on the stoop and gone on into the kitchen. Elly followed her inside. "I met a girl named Winnie in the ravine," she said. "Do you know her?"

Grandma shook her head. "I wonder who she is? There are so few children in the neighborhood anymore."

Elly ate her lunch and rested for a while, and later she ventured outside again. There had been something a little strange about Winnie, but Elly had liked her.

She'd be fun to play with. *If* she'd play with Elly now, after seeing her run away from the ravine like a baby.

But Winnie was nowhere to be found.

For the rest of the day, Elly wandered now and then to the back door, fingering the little necklace safe in her pocket and looking out at the garden. But no one was ever there.

She felt Grandma's anxious gaze at dinner and Grandpa made a lot of jokes while they played Scrabble. Elly tried to smile and joke back so they wouldn't worry.

It was a relief to go to bed at last, but then she was falling again and screaming "Mom!" again, and Grandma was at her bedside again, murmuring, "There, there, Elly, it's all right."

"Sorry, Grandma." Elly tried to smile. "I know I'm acting like a baby."

"Why, Elly." Grandma put her arm gently around Elly. "Nightmares are completely natural after what you've been through. I'm sure they'll stop soon."

I hope so, Elly thought as Grandma tucked her in. I hate the way I am now.

The next morning, she wandered around the house, tired already of the books and games she'd brought from home. She glanced outside a few times, but the backyard was always empty.

In the den, she picked up a school photograph of her cousin Kate. Short blonde hair, little freckled nose—Kate looked as tough and fearless as Elly used to be.

Elly looked at photographs of herself—her own school picture, one in ballet costume from last year's recital, one in mid-dive from the high board at last year's diving competition.

The high board. Her stomach fluttered, and she hastily put the photograph back on the table.

"Elly?" Grandma was calling.

Elly turned in relief from the photographs. "Here I am."

"I've just been talking to the nursing home," Grandma said. "Would you like to visit Gee Gee this afternoon? You've had a chance to rest, and she's been asking to see you."

Sweet old Gee Gee. Elly nodded. "I miss her," she said. "Maybe she can tell me something about my locket."

At the nursing home, they rode the elevator to the second floor. "I should warn you, Elly," Grandma whispered before she knocked. "Gee Gee's gotten a little forgetful. She's been much better lately, but she may not be quite the way you remember her."

Elly had just seen Gee Gee at Easter. How much could she have changed since then? she wondered as she followed Grandma into the room.

"Elly!" Gee Gee called instantly and held out her hands. She was sitting in the chair by the window, and except for wearing a robe and slippers, she looked the same as always, gray-haired, wrinkled, slim.

Elly moved across the room to kiss her great-great-aunt's cheek. "Hi, Gee Gee."

"Gee Gee?" The old woman sounded puzzled. Then she glanced past Elly and whispered, "Who's that old lady?"

Elly turned, bewildered. Gee Gee was pointing at Grandma—her niece, the woman she had raised as her own daughter.

"Elly, I'm sorry," Grandma murmured. "She's been so much better lately, that I thought . . ."

"Elly, sit down," Gee Gee said.

Why did Gee Gee know who she was, but not Grandma? Elly sat down, hesitantly fingering the necklace in her pocket and wishing Gee Gee would be the way she was supposed to be.

Grandma was trying to talk to Gee Gee about the garden when Gee Gee cut across her words. "What have you got there?" she asked Elly, her voice sharp.

Elly hadn't realized she'd taken the necklace out of her pocket. She held it up for Gee Gee to see. "Do you know—"

But Gee Gee snatched the necklace away before Elly finished her question. "The locket," Gee Gee said.

"Was it yours, Mama?" Grandma asked.

" 'Mama'?" Gee Gee repeated scornfully. "Who *is* that old lady?" she whispered to Elly.

Elly's heart sank. What was the matter with Gee Gee? She wasn't anything like Elly's sweet old aunt.

Elly watched the gnarled fingers rubbing the silver heart, over and over and over. Even if this strange Gee Gee did know something about the locket, would she ever be able to tell Elly?

"The clasp is crooked," Gee Gee said. "Who did it?"

4

Winnie Again

Grandpa fiddled with Elly's locket the next morning before he left for his office. "I've done what I can," he said, handing it to Elly, "but I'm afraid Grandma's right. A jeweler has to fix this."

Elly still knew nothing of the locket's past. Gee Gee had seemed confused and upset the longer they'd talked about it at the nursing home, so Grandma had changed the subject and she and Elly had left a little while later.

Now Elly glanced at Grandpa's handiwork. The clasp was much straighter, almost good as new. "Thanks, Grandpa," she said.

"I've got a good idea," Grandma said. "Let's stop at the jeweler's today, after we go out to lunch."

"Ah, the ladies who lunch," Grandpa teased from the back door. "Where are you going?"

Elly looked at him in mock indignation. "Grandpa! Where we always go: the Saratoga Hotel. It's tradition!"

Later, when she went upstairs to change, she thought about the annual lunch at the Saratoga. She and

Grandma always got dressed up, Elly always ordered the turkey club sandwich, Grandma always asked to see the pastry cart, and after lunch they always went to the ballet at the Saratoga Performing Arts Center.

But that was when she came for only a week in mid-July. Gloom descended on her as she stared into the closet. Today was the first day of July, and she was here for the whole summer. No ballet camp with her best friend Kim. No swim team. And the New York City Ballet wouldn't even be here for another week.

She gave herself a little shake. "Stop whining," she said aloud. "I'm better already." Last night when she'd had the nightmare, she hadn't screamed for Grandma. For the first time, she'd gone back to sleep on her own.

She pulled her Easter dress from the closet and slid it over her head. With its lace collar and old-fashioned style, it would have been perfect to wear with the locket.

Grandma wasn't ready yet. "I'll wait outside," Elly called. She slipped the necklace into her pocket to take to the jeweler's and went down the stairs and out into the sunshine.

Mindful of her good clothes, she sat down on the back step to wait for Grandma. She smoothed the skirt of her dress, running her hand over the necklace in her pocket. She could feel the chain, the little heart.

She slipped her hand into her pocket and pulled out the necklace. It lay gleaming on her palm. She rubbed her thumb over the tiny heart, smooth and warm. The locket was beautiful. It would be beautiful with her dresses.

She glanced at her reflection in the cellar window next to her, curious to see the locket against her dress.

She slipped it around her neck and carefully fastened the clasp.

Instantly everything swirled around her.

Dizzy! Dizzy again. She clutched the edge of the step as her head steadied. She hated this. She hated getting dizzy all the time and having nightmares. She hated being afraid.

Breathing deeply, she sat on the step, trying not to be discouraged. Getting better was going to take a long time, and she'd have to be patient.

"Elly!"

Winnie stood waving near the back of the garden. She must not be mad at her for running away. Relieved, Elly pushed aside her worries about herself and waved back.

She glanced at the back door. Grandma hadn't come down yet, and the dizziness was gone. Elly headed across the grass. At least she'd have time to apologize.

But Winnie didn't give her the chance. "Were you looking for me?" she asked. "I'm gathering leaves for my Impression Album. Have you made one yet?"

She *wasn't* mad. Happy, Elly peered at some leaves piled on the stone bench. "What's an Impression Album?"

Winnie stared at her. "All the girls are making them."

"Really? I've never heard of them." Elly picked up a small leaf. "What do you do with the leaves after you gather them?"

Winnie's face lit up with enthusiasm. "We print impressions of them, one to a page. Some of the older girls make beautiful pictures with twigs and blades of grass and tiny leaves. Helen started one, but—" She

25

broke off, and the look of sadness Elly remembered from the first day swept again over Winnie's face.

"Is Helen your friend who's in quarantine?" Elly asked.

Winnie shook her head. Her eyes were dark. "Helen died in April. She had scarlet fever too. Olivia's my friend in quarantine."

Elly drew in her breath. No wonder Winnie looked sad. Elly had never had a friend who had died.

Winnie jumped to her feet. "Let's go get some leaves for you. The ravine has lots of wildflowers."

The ravine. Even though Elly felt sorry for Winnie, her heart sank at the thought of the ravine. But she didn't want to look like a coward again, and she liked Winnie and her interesting ideas. Elly glanced toward the back door. Grandma still wasn't ready.

And Winnie was looking at her with pleading eyes. "Okay," Elly said, "but only for a little while."

The ravine was quiet and dark after the bright garden. The trees towering over the stream filtered the sunshine into gauzy light. Carefully, Elly followed Winnie, keeping her gaze on her feet.

"Look," Winnie said softly. She was bending over a small clump of greenery on one of the paths sloping down to the stream. "Lady's slippers."

Elly squatted next to her. Slender stalks bearing delicate pink flowers peeped from pointed green leaves. "They're pretty." But as Winnie gathered the flowers, memories of signs in other woods came to Elly. "Are you sure it's all right to pick them?" she asked. "They aren't an endangered species, are they?"

"What?" Winnie sat back on her heels and stared at Elly.

26

"You know, in danger of becoming extinct. Some wildflowers are."

"In danger of becoming extinct," Winnie repeated as if she couldn't believe her ears. "Wildflowers are all over! How could they become extinct? Look at the ravine!" She flung out her arms.

Everywhere the ground was carpeted with greenery. Elly frowned. "I guess it's all right."

"Of course it's all right," Winnie said. "Let's see what else we can find."

They picked little leaves and big ones, jagged leaves and smooth ones, round leaves and pointed ones. When they were done, they piled the leaves by the base of a huge tree.

Winnie brushed off her hands. "Now let's swing!"

Elly drew in her breath. "I don't think—my arm—"

"I'll help you. We can swing together, and we'll each hold on with one arm, and—"

"No." Elly's heart was pounding. "I can't. But I'll wait for you."

Winnie gave her a measuring look. "All right, but don't run away again."

Elly flushed. "I won't."

Winnie jumped for a spot high on the rope and swung out over the ravine.

Elly watched her go, hair streaming, dress flying. She forced her eyes to stay on Winnie—all the way to the other side and back—but she didn't look down and she made her mind go numb. No thoughts about rocks or falling—or Mom.

Winnie jumped off the rope. "How was that?"

"Great," Elly said with relief. She hadn't panicked.

Now she could at least watch Winnie swing without going crazy and running into the house for Grandma.

Grandma. "Oh, my gosh," Elly gasped. "My grandmother's waiting for me. I've got to go."

Winnie's face fell. "Oh, no! Can you come back tomorrow, same time?"

"Yes!" Elly called over her shoulder and hurried back through the bushes to the house. How long had she been gone? Grandma would be frantic. And her dress—

Elly tried to brush off the dirt on the hem. Now she'd have to change clothes.

And her locket! She had to take off the locket before Grandma noticed that she was wearing it. Elly reached up to the clasp and as the locket slid into her hands, she felt dizzy again, but she had to keep going. She stumbled up the back steps, slipping the necklace into her pocket. "Grandma!" she called. "I'm sorry! I—"

She halted just inside the kitchen. Grandma was coming into the room from the hall, checking through her handbag. "All ready, dear?" Grandma asked. "Sorry I kept you waiting."

Elly blinked. Grandma had kept her waiting? Elly shook her head, confused. "I'm sorry about my dress, Grandma," she said, reaching down to brush off the hem. But there was no dirt on her dress.

There was no dust on her shoes either, and her hands were clean. She looked up at Grandma in astonishment.

"Why? What's the matter with your dress, Elly?" Grandma asked. "I think it's lovely."

"Th-thank you," Elly stammered. "I thought it was dirty." She peered again at the hem, then at her hands. "But I guess it's not."

"Looks fine to me." Grandma tucked some tissues

into her handbag. "Have you got your locket, honey? I'll keep it in my purse until we get to the jewelry store."

Dazed, Elly handed the locket to Grandma and then followed her out to the car. She fastened the seat belt in silence as Grandma backed the car down the driveway. Had the dirt flown off her dress as she ran into the house?

She shook her head. That was stupid. But what had happened? She turned her hands over and looked at them in confusion.

"Something the matter, Elly?"

Had the accident affected her brain somehow? "No, Grandma. I'm fine."

"Well, good!" Grandma said cheerily. "We don't want anything to spoil our special lunch at the Saratoga. I'm trying to decide if I should order the Cobb salad or the spinach quiche. What do you think?"

Elly sat back and listened to Grandma chat about the menu at the restaurant. It was weird about her dress. She'd tell Winnie about it tomorrow.

She smiled to herself at the thought of having a friend here to tell things to. That would make the summer a little easier. Maybe Winnie had other ideas as interesting as that leaf album. She'd ask her tomorrow.

But Elly wasn't able to ask Winnie any questions the next day. Winnie didn't show up.

5

Something Very Strange

Winnie didn't show up the day after that either, not at eleven o'clock or any other time. Elly stood cautiously at the edge of the empty ravine, wondering what kind of a friend Winnie was. She had promised . . .

Elly sighed in disappointment. The summer was going to be very long without a friend.

She stepped carefully along the path toward the maple tree where she and Kate had built the fort. There were the old boards they'd nailed onto the trunk as steps. There, way up there, was the platform. Elly thought of climbing up the steps, standing on the platform, looking down into the ravine . . .

Her stomach dropped, and she turned away, disgusted with herself and lonely and wishing she were home with her parents and her friends.

The next day she sat in the kitchen, watching Grandma mix cookie dough. It was the Fourth of July, and there was nothing to do until the neighborhood pic-nic at two o'clock, three hours away.

Only eleven o'clock. She sighed and got up to wander around the kitchen. She nibbled at a spoonful of cookie dough from Grandma's big baking bowl. She sniffed Grandma's herbs growing in little pots on the window-sill above the sink. She ran her hand over the spines of Grandma's cookbooks sitting on the counter by the canisters.

Then she noticed a small jewelry box on the counter near the telephone. "Grandma, what's this?"

Grandma looked up from the cookie sheet. "Oh, Elly! I forgot. Mr. Schechter dropped that off last night."

Elly's spirits rose. Mr. Schechter was the jeweler to whom they'd taken the locket, and an old friend of Grandpa's. She flipped open the box. "Is it fixed?"

"Yup," Grandma said.

Elly carefully pulled the locket from the box. "It looks perfect," she breathed.

"Mr. Schechter thought it was quite old, but he couldn't say for sure," Grandma said.

"Can I wear it now?" Elly asked. "Can I wear it to the picnic?"

Grandma frowned. "I don't think that's a good idea, Elly. Why don't you save it for special occasions?"

"Okay," Elly said. But her fingers itched to put it around her neck. "I'll just see how it looks." She hur-ried into the little bathroom to use the mirror.

"Do you need help?" Grandma called.

"No, thanks," Elly said. Her arm was much better now. It didn't hurt at all when she raised it to fasten the locket behind her neck.

The clasp snicked into place, and instantly, Elly's head swam with dizziness. She grabbed onto the sink

31

to keep herself from falling, and groaned aloud. When would she be over these stupid dizzy spells?

With a sigh, she opened her eyes, and then she stared around her in alarm.

The sink she was clutching was a white pedestal sink, not Grandma's blue cabinet sink. The floor was made of tiny black and white tiles, not Grandma's blue linoleum, and the walls were covered with shiny white paint, not Grandma's blue-flowered wallpaper.

This was not Grandma's bathroom.

Elly's heart pounded with terror. Where was she? What had happened? She drew in her breath. Was she going crazy?

"Winnie!" someone called. "Winnie!"

Elly stumbled from the room and looked out the back door. A girl was running across the grass, followed by two boys. Winnie!

Eagerness to see Winnie again fought with Elly's questions about the strange room behind her. She glanced back at the door to the black and white bathroom, but the call came again.

"Winnie!"

Elly hesitated, torn, but when she saw Winnie disappearing into the bushes beyond the garden, she pushed open the back door.

In the ravine, Elly heard voices and, suddenly, there was Winnie and she wasn't alone. Several boys were with her, taking turns on the rope.

Elly forgot about the strange bathroom and stood still, watching. All but one of the four boys were bigger than Winnie. Were they all her brothers? Poor Winnie.

Winnie was trying to catch the rope for her turn,

but one of the boys grabbed it from her and swung, laughing, out over the ravine. "Edward!" she called angrily.

Stupid boys, Elly thought. They think they're so smart. But the kids at her school would laugh at those weird long shorts and funny leather shoes. She wondered if Winnie's family believed in a strange religion.

The boy named Edward came back on the rope, and another boy grabbed it away from Winnie. "It's my turn, James!" Winnie protested, but he only laughed and flew, yodeling, out over the rocks.

"Oh, let her have a turn," she heard one of the boys say. "Helen's gone, and Olivia's still in quarantine. She doesn't have anyone to play with."

"Thanks, Gil," Winnie said, and Elly watched her jump to get a hold on the rope and swing out over the ravine. But the biggest boy gestured to the others, and they all ran off down one of the paths.

Winnie came swinging back. "Hello! I'm glad to see you."

Elly smiled back. "I'm glad to see *you*. But where have you been? I thought we were going to meet each other two days ago."

"I was here."

"I couldn't find you. I came yesterday and the day before."

"I couldn't find *you!* Oh, well." Winnie smiled again. "At least you're here now. The boys have been horrible."

"Are they your brothers?"

Winnie made a face. "Three are. The other one's Gil, their friend. Sometimes he's nice." She paused, measuring Elly with her eyes. Then, as if she'd made a decision, she said, "Come on. I want to show you something."

"What?" Elly asked.

But Winnie just smiled and gestured for Elly to follow.

Elly hoped Winnie didn't want to show her something high off the ground, but before she could decide what to say, Winnie was heading down the path to the bottom of the ravine. Elly swallowed. I can do it, she told herself.

Stepping slowly and keeping her gaze on her feet, she made her way downward, clutching at bushes and branches and even weeds until finally she was at the bottom.

Breathing deeply, she paused and looked around. She'd made it!

Birds called faintly overhead, and at her feet the little stream tinkled. But there was no sound of the boys. The ravine was hushed and shadowed and still.

Winnie spoke in a whisper. "This way," she said, and led Elly along a path bordering the little stream. At last she halted near some bushes, listened intently, then stooped, drew aside a branch, and crawled into the bushes.

Wondering, Elly crawled after her and discovered that the bushes had been hollowed out like tunnels. One bush led to another, which led to another, and in the center was a place large enough for the two of them to sit. Overhead, the branches had grown together to form a roof.

"Wow," she breathed. "What a wonderful place." It was cozy, protected, safe.

Winnie had been watching her anxiously, and now she smiled. "I thought you would like it."

"This would make a great hideout," Elly said. "Do your brothers know about it?"

Winnie made a fierce face. "No! And they never will!" Then she smiled as if Elly had passed a test. "You and I could meet here every day. My mother has a little bit of carpet I could have for the floor—"

"I bet my grandma would let me have some old dishes," Elly said. "And we could bring food . . ."

"And books!"

"And paper and pencils!"

"We could draw and write stories . . ."

"Or plays . . ."

They grinned at each other and excitedly made plans. Then Winnie got to her knees. "Come on, let's explore!"

Uh oh. But maybe their exploring could keep them at the bottom of the ravine.

"Okay," Elly said, crawling out of the hideout after Winnie. "How far does the little stream go?"

Winnie pointed upstream. "That way it ends in Dutchman's Park, but I've never followed it very far the other way."

Elly put her hand on Winnie's shoulder and turned her to face downstream. "Let's find out then!"

They wandered along the path, discovering little trails and pretty stones and small patches of wildflowers. They went under an old stone bridge and listened to strange clopping sounds over their heads.

"That must be Schuyler Street," Winnie said. "Which means we must be close to the college, and that's where the stream ends."

"Wow," Elly said. The college was blocks away from Grandma's house.

Winnie turned. "We'd better head back. Oh my, look at that." She pointed to a collection of old boards and rocks at the base of the bridge. "I wonder if that's the fort I hear the boys talking about."

That reminded Elly of the fort she and Kate had built last summer. "Now it's my turn to show *you* something," she said before she could lose her nerve.

"What do you want to show me?" Winnie asked.

Elly wouldn't have to climb into the fort she and Kate had built last summer. She could just point it out. "Come on," she said. They worked their way back along the stream to a spot behind Grandma's house, and then Elly led the way up the slope.

She followed the path along the top of the ravine, again keeping her gaze on her feet, and then stopped abruptly.

She looked around in confusion. "Where is it?"

"Where's what?" Winnie asked, gazing around too. "What are you looking for?"

"Our fort. Kate's and my tree fort." Elly stared at the spot where the maple tree should have been. Not only was the fort gone, so was the maple tree.

"Who's Kate?" Winnie asked.

Elly didn't answer. She squatted and peered at the ground. There was no hole, there were no roots, there was nothing to indicate that a tree of any kind had ever been in that spot.

She stood up, frowning. Was she in the wrong place? The fort had been here just yesterday when she'd been waiting for Winnie.

36

Elly gazed up and down the path. There was the trail to Grandma's honeysuckle bushes. There was the path down to the stream. And here, right here where she stood, was the place for the maple tree and the fort.

But they weren't there.

6

Questions

"Elly, is something the matter?" Winnie asked.

Elly fought down a sense of panic. So many weird things were happening—finding herself in that strange room, the dirt disappearing from her dress, and now the fort vanishing. "I don't understand," she said.

"Winnie!" A call came faintly from beyond the honeysuckle bushes.

"That's my brother," Winnie said. "I must go— we're going to the parade downtown. Can you meet me again tomorrow?"

"Yes. Okay." Still bewildered, Elly followed Winnie back along the path and through the honeysuckle bushes.

"Good." Winnie flashed a smile at her. "See you then. Coming!" she called in answer to a second "Winnie!" and ran lightly across the grass and into Grandma's house.

Into Grandma's house! Elly stood dumbstruck, staring at the back door. Why had Winnie run into Grandma's house? Did she know Elly's grandmother?

Without another thought, Elly followed, racing across the lawn and up the back steps to the kitchen door.

And she entered a kitchen she had never seen before.

She stared in shock. A huge black stove crouched against one wall. An old-fashioned sink hung from the wall under the window, and a scrubbed pine table sat in the middle of the room. The far wall held only two cupboards.

She glanced back at the door she had just come through. It looked like Grandma's door. The view through the screen looked like the view of Grandma's back yard.

But this was not Grandma's kitchen.

She edged toward the back hall. What was this place? Had she somehow walked into the wrong house? But that was impossible! She had followed Winnie into Grandma's house!

Winnie! Where was she? Where had she gone?

Voices came rapidly toward the kitchen from what must be the front hall. Adult voices. Elly froze. Who were they? What would they say if they found her here? A door stood open beside her, and she ducked behind it.

And she found herself in the strange bathroom she had been in earlier. She stared at the tiny black and white tiles and the white pedestal sink.

Footsteps sounded in the kitchen, and her heart thudded. What if someone came in here? She looked wildly around for a way out, but there was none. She was trapped.

The footsteps stopped outside the door. She backed up against the sink, nervously fingering the chain of the locket. Don't come in! she wanted to cry.

Someone rattled the door knob. The knob turned. The door began to open.

"No!" she screamed. And then her head was swirling and she was crying out and grabbing for the sink as if it were a lifeline.

"Elly?" came Grandma's voice outside the bathroom. "Are you all right?"

Grandma! Elly opened her eyes. She was back in Grandma's bathroom. She flung open the door. "Grandma!"

"Elly, what's the matter?" Grandma guided her to the kitchen table. "Sit down, honey. Were you dizzy again?"

"Oh, Grandma." How could Elly explain what had happened? She sank into a chair and put her head in her hand. What *had* happened? Was her dizziness getting worse? And that weird place . . . It had been like a dream in the middle of the day.

"Eleanor, we forgot all about the parade!" Grandpa hurried into the kitchen, then paused as he noticed Elly. "What's the matter, honey?"

Elly tried to smile. "I'm okay." She didn't want them to worry about her. "What's this about a parade?" Winnie had been going to a parade.

"No parade for you, Elly," Grandma said. "I think you'd better rest for a while."

Grandpa glanced at the clock. "Besides," he said, "we'd never get across the river in time."

Eleven o'clock! It had been eleven o'clock hours ago when Elly had first gone into the bathroom to try on the locket.

Then something else Grandpa had said sunk in. "Across the river?" Elly repeated. "Isn't the parade downtown?'' Winnie had said she was going downtown to see the parade.

Grandpa shook his head with a smile. ''There hasn't been a Fourth of July parade downtown since I was a boy.''

Since Grandpa was a boy! Panic rose inside Elly like a wave. What was going on? Was her concussion making her see things—and hear things—that weren't real? Had her brain been damaged? What was wrong?

She reached up to rub the heart of the locket—It was gone! ''Grandma! I've lost my locket!'' Hadn't she fastened it tightly? Had she lost it in the ravine? *Every*thing was wrong.

''Shhh, Elly.'' Grandma left her side for a moment, then returned. ''Here it is. You must have dropped it in the bathroom.''

''Oh, Grandma. Thanks.'' Elly inspected the locket, closed its clasp, then curled her fingers around it. At least the locket was all right. She glanced up and caught her grandparents exchanging worried looks.

A chill went through her. They thought something was wrong with her, too.

Rain pattering against the window woke Elly the next morning. She dressed slowly, looking out at the rain, then went downstairs for breakfast. Grandma had insisted yesterday that Elly should rest, so they'd missed both the picnic and the fireworks.

But even though Elly had had all that time to be quiet and to think, all she came up with were questions.

Questions about the strange house, questions about the missing tree fort, questions about the kitchen clock—questions that had no answers.

41

Down in the kitchen, she looked out the window at the wet garden. If only she could go outside. Maybe Winnie could help her.

But the rain did not stop, and the day passed slowly. Elly spent the morning reading old books that had belonged to her mother as a child—*The Secret Garden, The Blue Fairy Book,* even some ancient Nancy Drews. She ate lunch. She played five games of gin rummy with Grandma. She tossed balls for the cat to chase and rearranged the china angels on Gee Gee's dresser and rested for a while in her room.

But, every now and then, memories of the strange things that had happened yesterday flashed into her mind, followed by the worst question of all: was something really wrong with her?

After her rest, the fragrance of baking bread drew her downstairs. Two loaves of freshly-baked bread sat cooling on a rack. "Mmm. Smells good, Grandma."

"Would you like a piece? It's cool enough to slice."

"Yes, please." Elly sat down at the table. A book with a photograph of an old-fashioned house on the cover lay next to Grandma's coffee mug.

"My neighbor wrote that book, Elly," Grandma said. "It's about our neighborhood. You might like to take a look at it."

Elly pulled the book closer. *College Hill: Turn Of The Century Elegance* was the title. "Hmmm," she said politely, hoping Grandma didn't expect her to read it.

But then she noticed the people in the photograph. A group of children stood formally at the base of the wide front steps, staring into the camera. The boys wore weird long shorts, and all the girls were dressed exactly like Winnie.

She stared at the photograph. The girls all wore dark tights and low-waisted dresses like Winnie's, and two of them had their hair pulled back with big bows like Winnie sometimes wore.

She looked again at the title. "Turn of the century" meant the end of the 1800s and the beginning of the 1900s. Why did Winnie wear clothes from 1900?

Did her family believe in a strange religion that made them wear old-fashioned clothes, or . . .

Was Winnie really *from* that time?

Was Winnie a ghost?

7

Ghosts?

Elly stared at the photograph. Was it possible? Winnie—a ghost?

But that was crazy! Winnie was real. She was Elly's friend. Besides, everyone knew there was no such thing as ghosts.

Still . . . Elly's mind was whirling. It would explain so many things. How Winnie could go to a parade that hadn't existed for fifty years. Why she didn't know about wildflowers being endangered and why she wore dresses and tights and bows in her hair just to play in the ravine.

"Elly?" Grandma was holding out a plate of bread and butter.

"Sorry, Grandma. I must have been daydreaming." Elly accepted the plate and took a bite of the fresh bread, but she kept thinking about ghosts. In all the ghost stories she'd read, ghosts haunted people for a reason. To right a wrong. To save someone from harm. Or . . .

Because something horrible had happened to them, and their spirits could not rest. Had something horrible happened to Winnie? Did she need Elly's help?

Grandma handed her a glass of milk and then sat at the table with a fresh cup of coffee.

"Thanks, Grandma." Elly took a sip of milk, and then more questions crowded her mind. She'd first met Winnie in the garden. Was the garden haunted? The ravine? Her grandmother's house? What about those weird rooms?

"Say, Grandma . . ." She tried to sound merely curious. "Have you heard of any houses around here with ghosts?"

"Goodness. Ghosts? Well . . ." Grandma looked thoughtful. "There are some famous houses in the neighborhood. A governor of the state was born in a house on Park Street, and . . . hmmm . . ." She nodded at the book on the table. "There might be some interesting things in there."

"What about this house?" Elly asked. "Any ghosts here?" She gave a little laugh. She didn't want to sound as if she believed in ghosts.

Grandma smiled. "Not that I know of." She reached for the book and opened it. "Did you see the picture of our house?"

Elly's breath caught. Maybe there was a photograph of Winnie in Grandma's book!

"Here we are." Grandma was pointing to a picture of the familiar square frame house. Elly's heart jumped, but there were no people in the photograph.

"Hmmm," Elly said, her heart still pounding, and held out her hand. "May I look?"

45

"Of course." Grandma handed her the book. "I didn't know you were interested in history, Elly."

Elly glanced up from her quick perusal of the first pages. "Well . . ."

But Grandma was beaming. "I've got a wonderful idea. Let's do a family tree this summer. Wouldn't that be fun?"

Oh, no. All Elly had wanted to know about was ghosts. "Sure," she said, hoping Grandma would forget about it.

"We'll call it the Eleanor Tree." Grandma looked enthusiastic. "Instead of concentrating on the last name—which is what you usually do in a family tree—we'll focus on the women named Eleanor."

"Okay." Maybe the family tree would go quickly without sons or brothers. Elly thought of Winnie's brothers. If Winnie were a ghost, they must be ghosts, too.

A shiver slid deliciously down her spine. Ghosts, a haunted ravine . . . She felt like the old adventurous Elly. She couldn't wait until the rain stopped so she could go out to the garden and find Winnie again.

Elly returned to the book, but although she examined each photograph carefully, she found no picture of Winnie.

Too bad. That would have been really exciting.

That evening, as the rain continued, Elly tried to write a letter to her best friend Kim back home. But it was no good. All she wanted to tell her about was Winnie, and she couldn't find the right words.

She sat at the Eleanor desk in her room, crumpled papers at her feet, and wished she could talk to her mother. But even understanding Mom might not believe in Elly's ghost.

What about her cousin Kate? Elly closed the desk and went downstairs. Her grandparents were in the little den, watching the news. "Grandma, would it be all right if I called Kate?"

"What are you going to call her?" Grandpa asked.

"Oh, Grandpa!" Elly gave him a gentle poke in the arm.

Grandma gave permission, and Elly went into the sunroom to make her call. She closed the French doors and punched in Kate's number.

But Kate wasn't home, and there was no one else to call. Elly went to bed without having told anyone about her ghosts.

The nightmare, as usual, woke her in the middle of the night. But she went back to sleep easily, thinking about ghosts, and the next morning when she awoke she found that the rain had stopped during the night.

She looked carefully out her window and saw mist hovering along the grass and fog shrouding the honeysuckle bushes at the back of the garden. Any hint of the ravine had vanished.

A ghostly fog, she thought, tingling with anticipation, and pulled on some clothes. She scooped her locket off the nightstand and hurried out of the room.

Downstairs, the kitchen was empty. She left a note for her grandparents, tiptoed across the linoleum to the back door, and slipped outside to the stone bench.

She hoped Winnie wouldn't take too long. "Winnie!" she called softly, not wanting to awaken anyone. "Winnie!"

But Winnie didn't come. Elly waited and waited, fiddling with the necklace in her pocket. She hoped this wouldn't be another one of those times when Winnie didn't show up.

She went into the ravine and looked, but she could see no one in the fog and Winnie didn't answer her calls. She went back to the stone bench. She fidgeted with the necklace in her pocket, drew it out, and decided to wear it. She'd be careful. She reached up and clasped it around her neck.

Dizziness swirled over her, and she grabbed onto the bench to steady herself. Dizzy again!

Wait a minute. The sudden thought electrified her. Was the locket making her dizzy? Not the accident?

She remembered other times she'd fastened or unfastened the locket . . . on the stone bench, at the back steps, in that weird bathroom . . .

She reached up and took off the locket. Dizzy. She put the locket back on. Dizzy again.

She could feel a smile growing across her face. It *was* the locket. It wasn't her head. *She* was all right.

Relief washed over her. She was all right! A locket making her dizzy was weird, but no weirder than Winnie's being a ghost. Elly's smile widened, and, feeling as light as air, she went looking again for Winnie.

Mist filled the ravine. It drifted around tree trunks, disguised familiar landmarks, and hid the rocks at the bottom.

Elly shivered with delight. It looked enchanted. Or haunted. She smiled to herself. She *was* the old Elly. Bring on the ghosts!

"Boo!" said a voice behind her.

She whirled. Winnie stood on the path, grinning at her.

"I didn't hear you!" Elly said. Was Winnie always this quiet? Ghosts were supposed to glide silently about.

"She went this way!" came a voice from farther back in the mist.

"Quick!" Winnie whispered, putting a finger to her lips. She pulled Elly behind a tree, and within seconds a bunch of boys thundered past.

Winnie's brothers. Elly recognized them. But if they were ghosts, they made a lot of noise.

"Follow me!" Winnie ordered in a whisper and moved swiftly down the path. There was no time for questions. Elly hurried after her.

Then, ahead of them in the fog, one of the boys said, "Hold up, James."

Elly and Winnie halted, crouching behind a bush. Elly could hear the boys conferring in loud whispers. Winnie tapped Elly's arm, mouthing, "Watch this." "Ohhhhhhh," Winnie moaned. "Ohhhhh."

"What was that?" Elly heard one of the boys say.

"That didn't sound like Winnie," a young voice quavered.

"Of course that was Winnie," someone else said, sounding disgusted.

Winnie giggled, picked up a rock and heaved it into the ravine.

"She's down there!"

"Come on!"

Feet pounded, twigs cracked, grunts sounded. "Ow! Eddie!" someone complained.

Winnie's eyes shone. Elly giggled and clapped a hand over her mouth. Winnie beckoned, and they crept down the ravine toward the noise.

But when they got to the bottom, there was silence.

Mist swam at their feet. Tree branches poked out of the fog like ghostly fingers. Even the sound of the little stream bubbling over stones was muffled.

"Eddie, wait for me," a voice whined.

"Shhh!" one of the boys said.

Winnie grinned and nodded her head upstream toward the voices. Elly followed her silently up the path. Step after quiet step, they moved slowly through the fog. Elly could see only Winnie's back in front of her.

Then someone jumped out at them from behind a tree. "Boooooo!"

Elly screamed. Winnie screamed. More boys jumped onto the path, shouting and laughing. "We got you!" "We won! We won!"

Winnie laughed and so did Elly, and the boys punched each other in the shoulder. "We did it!" "We tricked her!"

"All right, you guys," Elly said, but no one looked at her. "Hey!" But the boys kept laughing and shouting and punching each other.

Elly frowned at Winnie, then tried again. "HEY!" This time she shouted, but no one even turned.

They hadn't heard her! The hair rose on the back of her neck. They hadn't heard her or seen her. She was invisible to them.

Suddenly, she was terrified. Winnie could see her. Why couldn't they? She whirled and ran, down the path, away from the boys, away from Winnie, away from all the things she didn't understand.

Footsteps pounded behind her. "Elly!" Winnie called. "Wait!"

Elly slowed. *Winnie* had seen her. She had always seen her.

"Elly!" Winnie called again, and Elly stopped and waited.

"Why did you run off?" Winnie said. "Wasn't that fun? We'll get them next time!"

Elly stared at her, trying to figure it all out. "Let's talk in the hideout," she said and silently led the way along the path.

In the hideout, she sat cross-legged on the carpet and looked at Winnie. She took a deep breath. "Are you a ghost?"

"Me?" Winnie laughed. "No! You are!"

Elly was a ghost? She was shocked into silence. Was that why the boys hadn't seen her?

No. That couldn't be the answer, because ghosts were the spirits of people who were dead, and she wasn't dead.

But if Winnie wasn't a ghost ... Elly thought hard, remembering the strange things that had happened yesterday. The fort disappearing ... the kitchen clock standing still ... the old-fashioned rooms ...

Her breath caught. Rooms as old-fashioned as Winnie's clothing ... Time standing still ... Was it possible ... ?

She glanced down at the locket lying on her tee-shirt. The locket. The *locket*. Maybe the locket did more than make her dizzy.

"Winnie ..." she said slowly, trying to find the right words. "What's today's date?"

"July sixth."

"I know, but what year?" Elly held her breath.

Winnie frowned. "Nineteen twelve, silly."

1912! Elly's breath burst out. She was right! "Winnie," she whispered. "It's time travel. I live in the future—your future.'' The locket was magic—a magical instrument of time travel.

"Time travel?" Winnie repeated.

Elly nodded. "Watch." She reached up to the clasp of the locket. "Tell me what happens when I take this off. Tell me if I disappear."

The locket slid into Elly's hands, her head swam, and when she opened her eyes, Winnie was gone.

Elly stared around her, awestruck. Not only Winnie was gone. The little carpet was gone. Winnie's pile of leaves was gone. Even the tangled bushes of the hideout were gone.

Elly was sitting alone in the middle of a dirt path at the bottom of the ravine, as scraps of mist floated eerily about her. High overhead, birds called faintly to one another, and shafts of sunlight came slanting into the ravine to chase away the mist.

She rubbed her fingers across the ground—dirt, stones, little bits of greenery. The stones sifted through her fingers, and she realized with a shock that none of these things—the stones, the birds, maybe even the dirt—had been in Winnie's ravine. They couldn't have been, because Winnie's ravine was from more than eighty years ago.

Eighty years ago. Elly shook her head in amazement. She reached up to fasten the locket again, and then she heard Grandma's voice.

"Elly!"

Oh, no. Elly's fingers froze. Not now. She had to get back to Winnie and tell her what had happened.

"Elly!" Grandma's voice came closer. "Where are you?"

She sounded anxious. Elly didn't want Grandma to

worry about her. "Coming!" she called, and headed for the slope. She'd see what Grandma wanted and then hurry back.

Her head whirled with questions as she struggled up out of the ravine. Of course she'd read books about time travel, but she'd never thought *she* would travel to another time.

What did Winnie think? Did she even know about time travel? Elly couldn't wait to talk to her. Was there any way to get Winnie into her own time?

"Elly! There you are." Grandma stood just at the edge of the ravine. "Come quickly, dear. Your dad's on the phone. He's coming for a visit this afternoon."

8

Magic

Fear that Dad's phone call meant Mom was worse drove every other thought from Elly's head. But Dad's voice was reassuring.

"Mom is doing well," he said, "so well that I can take a day to come and see you. How are you? Grandma says you're much better, too."

Elly sighed with relief. "Yup," she said. Except for the nightmares, that was true. Her bruises were healing, and her arm didn't hurt anymore. And now there was Winnie . . . Elly slipped her hand into her pocket and touched the chain of the necklace.

"Good," Dad said, breaking into her thoughts. "I'll see you this afternoon. Tell Grandma that I'm looking forward to that strawberry pie. I love you, honey."

"I love you, Dad."

Grandma wouldn't let Elly go back outside without eating breakfast, and suddenly Elly realized she was starving. She dug into the oatmeal Grandma had cooked for her, and the grapefruit and the blueberry muffins—

and looked around Grandma's kitchen in wonder. That other kitchen must have been Winnie's kitchen in 1912. 1912 ... Elly hadn't known Grandma's house was that old.

She finished eating, stacked her dishes in the dishwasher, and slipped out the back door. The sun had burned off most of the mist in the garden, but little wisps of fog still floated through the ravine.

She stood at the top, well back from the edge, and pulled the locket from her shorts. She held her breath and fastened the clasp, and her head spun.

Dizzy, from crossing into another time. Elly shivered with delight as she gazed around the ravine. It was true. The trees were different and the bushes and—she turned to look for the tree fort. Yes. The tree fort was gone— and so was the tree.

"I'm really in nineteen twelve," she whispered to herself. Then, slowly, averting her eyes from the bottom of the ravine, she moved down the slope.

"Win," she called softly. "Winnie!" She reached the little stream and followed the path to the tunneled-out bushes of the hideout. "Winnie," she called again. But Winnie did not answer.

Elly listened intently. Birds called to each other high overhead, the little stream bubbled nearby, but there was no sound of children. She glanced at her watch. Winnie must be having breakfast.

Or was the time of day different in Winnie's time? Elly thought for a moment. Whenever she'd been with Winnie, shadows and sunshine seemed to have been the same. Even the fog had been the same.

When would Winnie return? Maybe she had chores

to do . . . What did girls do in 1912? Elly had so many questions . . .

Maybe Winnie was waiting on the stone bench. But the garden was empty, and now Elly saw that this was a different garden. Peonies grew in the same place, but not Grandma's new dark red peonies, and the marigolds were missing.

She crept forward across the grass toward the house. Could she see inside through the windows? No. Too high. But the curtains were different from Grandma's.

She moved along the house toward the driveway and peered past huge bushes shielding the garage. But the garage was gone. In its place was a two-story building with huge doors. One of the doors was open, and there was a smell, a barn-like smell.

Inside, two horses stood in stalls, and there was a carriage or a buggy of some sort. She stood at the door, staring. It was a carriage house. Winnie's family had had horses and a carriage.

Elly turned to look past the house toward the street. Were horses and buggies going down the street even now? Or trolleys? Or people dressed in old-fashioned clothes? She had to see.

She moved down the dirt driveway and out to the front of the house. The towering shade trees of Grandma's neighborhood were gone, and the houses all looked new. She gazed at their bright paintwork and straight porches and shining windows.

And the street . . . it wasn't the black asphalt Elly was used to, but bumpy, lumpy brick. Was that what Winnie rode her bike on? Did kids *have* bikes in 1912?

A strange clopping noise sounded at her back. Elly

whirled. A horse pulling a buggy was trotting down the street towards her. A horse and buggy!

She shrank back instinctively and watched them pass. The horse was huge, the buggy bumped along the bricks, and the driver was a man with a funny cap and mustache.

She shook her head in amazement. She really was in 1912. She couldn't wait to explore with Winnie. There was so much to see.

At last, she turned and headed back down the driveway, past the strange old barn, back to the bench in the garden. That was the only thing that was the same. Bushes were in the wrong places. A tree grew where there was none in her time, and the curtains on the back windows of the house were lacy-looking instead of plain.

Where was Winnie? Elly couldn't wait to talk everything over with Winnie.

But Grandma thought Elly looked pale, and she made her rest quietly until dinnertime. Then Dad arrived, with hugs for Elly and good news about Mom. "Only one of her legs needs surgery," he said. "The other one is healing already."

"That's wonderful," Grandma said. "How's the pain?"

Dad hesitated. "Better, I guess, but she's still on a lot of medication."

Elly pictured Mom covered with bruises and bandages, the way she had been the day Elly left the hospital. "I wish I could talk to her."

Dad put his arm around her. "Let's call her tonight."

After dinner, Dad and Elly went into the sunroom,

and Dad dialed Mom's number at the hospital. "Remember, she's taking a lot of pain medicine," he said to Elly. "She'll sound a little different to you."

Elly nodded but when she heard her mother's voice, she was shocked. It didn't sound like Mom at all.

"Hi, honey," Mom said, just as she always did, but her voice was weak and fuzzy.

"Hi, Mom," Elly said. "How are you?"

"Fine," Mom said. "How are you?" But Mom didn't sound fine to Elly. They talked for just a few minutes, Dad spoke briefly to Mom, and then the call was over.

Elly looked at her father. "Oh, Dad," she said.

"Come on, Elly," he said. "Let's go for a walk."

The evening was warm. Golden sunlight slanted through the branches of the big trees lining the street. Elly walked down the sidewalk with her father, glad to be with him, but worrying about Mom. Would she be all right? If only Elly had done something that day to help her . . .

Dad seemed to sense her anxiety. "She's a fighter, Elly, you know that."

Elly nodded. That was true.

"And she's getting better every day. Before you know it, she'll sound just like your old Mom."

Elly studied her father's face. "Really, Dad?"

"Really, Elly. We just have to be patient."

Elly felt a little better.

"So," Dad asked, glancing at her, "how's my other injured girl? How's the arm?"

"Pretty good."

"Still having nightmares?"

Elly hesitated. "Sometimes." Every night still, but she didn't want to add to Dad's worries.

He put a hand on her shoulder. "They'll go away. We have to be patient about that, too."

Elly smiled then, comforted, and Dad changed the subject. "What a beautiful old neighborhood this is."

For the first time since they'd started walking, Elly stopped worrying about Mom. She looked at the houses they were passing, big old houses that must have been around in 1912, and she thought of Winnie. Had she been inside that green house? Had she had a friend who lived in that brown one?

She'd probably never seen anyone like the woman in shorts and tank top jogging down the street. Elly was struck by how much things must have changed since 1912.

"Dad ..." she began hesitantly. She had so many questions about the locket and about Winnie, and Dad was always good to talk to. He read a lot of science fiction ... but would he believe her? "Dad, what do you think about time travel?"

He grinned at her. "What have you been reading? *The Time Machine?*"

She grinned back. That had been the wrong thing to say. "Oh, I don't know. I just was thinking about these old houses, and wondering if, you know, somehow ..." She searched for the right words. "Maybe the people who lived in them, say eighty years ago, are still there? On another level of time ... like, sort of, a loop?" She gave a little laugh. She didn't want him to think she believed in time travel.

"Hmmmm." Dad looked thoughtful. "That's an interesting idea. And, if you could find the mechanism, you could go from loop to loop?''

''Yeah.'' Was that what was happening with her and Winnie?

''Sounds great. I'd like to go looping through time. But—here's an interesting question. If you had the choice, would you go back in time or forward?''

Elly smiled to herself. That was one of Dad's favorite ''interesting questions.'' They had talked about it at dinner more than once. Dad always chose the future, Mom always chose the past, and Elly sometimes chose one, sometimes the other.

Today it was easy to choose. ''I'd go back in time,'' she said. Back to 1912.

9

Plastic

The next morning, after Dad had left for his drive back to the hospital, Elly slipped out to the garden, the locket in her hand.

In the ravine, she stood carefully back from the edge of the path, then jeered at herself. Terrified of heights, but willing to travel through time—that made no sense.

She clasped the locket together and waited for the dizziness to pass. "Winnie!" she called softly. "Winnie!" But there was no answer.

Cautiously grabbing onto bushes as she went, she made her way down the path and into the hideout. But no one was there.

Elly dug into her pocket and pulled out the pen, paper, and plastic sandwich bag she had gathered from Grandma's kitchen. "Dear Winnie, Where are you?" she wrote. "Wait for me here or leave me a message. We have a lot to talk about! Love, Elly."

She read over the note, then added a few lines. "P.S.

Since I'm invisible to your brothers, I can spy on them for you!''

She folded the piece of paper, wrote WINNIE in large letters on the outside, then slipped it into the plastic sandwich bag. She laid it on a corner of the old carpet, weighted it down with a heavy rock, and headed back up the ravine.

At the top, she hesitated at the sight of the tree with the rope swing. She touched the rope, looped over a branch. She forced herself to look up, way, way up to the limb it hung from, and then across to the other side of the ravine. But she could not force herself to look down onto the rocks.

Afraid. She was still afraid.

Grandma wanted to begin the Eleanor Tree that afternoon. ''Here we are,'' she said happily. ''Family bible, old photographs, letters.''

Elly's heart sank as she glanced at the stuff Grandma had collected. The Eleanor Tree looked like a lot of work.

But it turned out to be more interesting than she had expected. First, Grandma opened up the old Bible to the ''Births'' page and showed Elly her own name: ''Eleanor Anne Morrison.''

''That's me!'' Elly said, pleased. Right above her name was Kate's—Katharine Eleanor Broughton—and right below was Elly's cousin Robbie's. The first name on the page had been written in flowing handwriting: Jeremiah Hamilton, born 1871.

''Wow,'' Elly said. ''This is old.'' She peered at the names at the top of the page. ''Who was the first Eleanor?''

"My great-aunt, Nellie Ashe," Grandma said. "She was Jeremiah's sister."

"Nellie!" Elly exclaimed. "Ugh."

Grandma laughed and handed Elly a piece of paper. "We'll start with you," she said, "instead of Nellie. Write your name at the top and your date of birth."

That was easy. After her name came Mom's: Eleanor Jane Broughton, and then Grandma's: Eleanor Ruth Gilbert. Then Elly's eye was caught by the photograph on the top of a pile of old pictures.

A young-looking Mom was sitting on the stone bench in Grandma's back yard, and on her lap was Elly as a baby.

Mom. Grief washed over Elly. Why hadn't she grabbed her mother as she was slipping? Why had she stood there—*frozen*—as Mom fell and fell and fell and—

"I've got to get these photographs organized," Grandma was saying. "Maybe I'll do it while you're here this summer. Would you like to help me? Elly?"

Elly struggled to pull her thoughts from Mom. "Sure," she said and tried to smile.

"Now, who do you suppose was the Eleanor before me?" Grandma asked. "Remember, it wasn't my mother . . ."

Elly knew Grandma was trying to distract her from thinking about Mom, but she couldn't help remembering that Grandma's own mother had died as a young woman. "What *was* your mother's name?" Elly asked softly. Poor Grandma. Losing your mother was about the worst thing that could happen to you. Elly would never forget how pale and still Mom had been, lying on the rocks.

"Florence," Grandma said. "I was only two when my parents died, though, so I don't remember them at all." She paused, then patted Elly's hand. "It's all right, Elly. Everything will be all right."

Elly felt a little better. She looked up at Grandma and gave her a real smile.

Grandma smiled back. "Now, who *was* the Eleanor before me?"

Elly didn't have to look. "Gee Gee," she said. Gee Gee, who had taken in her sister's baby and raised her as her own daughter. Grandma had always called her "Mama," and Elly had always called her "Gee Gee."

Grandpa poked his head into the sunroom. "How are all you Eleanors doing?"

"Just fine," Elly said. "Look, Grandpa." She held up the page on which she'd written three names and birth dates.

Grandpa feigned disbelief. "All that gabbing, and that's all you've done?"

"We've made a good beginning," Grandma told Grandpa. "Right, Elly?"

Elly nodded. "And just think, Grandpa," she said. "The next names in this Bible might be *my* children's. Maybe there'll be another Eleanor."

"Not another Eleanor!" Grandpa joked, putting up his hands as if to protect himself. "How many Eleanors can a person take?"

"Grandpa!" Elly grinned at him.

"Want to take a walk before supper?" he said.

"Uh oh." Grandma glanced at her watch. "The potatoes! Elly, we'll work on this again another day."

Grandma hurried into the kitchen then, and Elly went outside with Grandpa. If she did have a daughter and named her Eleanor, she mused as she strolled down the street, what would she call her for a nickname? Not Nellie, that's for sure.

She waited until the next morning to try again to find Winnie. As she slipped out to the garden, full of sunshine and singing birds, an alarming thought came to her. Maybe Winnie was afraid. She'd seemed to be the kind of girl who would like adventure, but Elly's disappearance might have scared her.

The ravine was dark and shadowy. Elly found her way to the bottom in her usual fashion, keeping her gaze on her feet, grabbing at branches and bushes to slow her down, and trying the whole time not to think about falling.

When she was safely at the bottom, she fastened the locket around her neck and waited for the dizziness to pass, then moved quietly along the path to the hideout. She crawled in, and there was Winnie.

"Hello!" Winnie grinned. She didn't look frightened.

"You're not scared of me," Elly said in relief.

"Scared? Not me!" Winnie said. "I want to hear all about this time travel. You disappeared!"

Elly grinned back. She told Winnie what she had figured out about the locket and then explained that Grandma had called her away from the ravine. "And when I came back, you were gone."

"We had to visit my aunt and uncle." With a sly smile, Winnie held up Elly's note. "Can you really spy on the boys for me?"

"Why not?" Elly said. "I guess they can't see me, so I can find out whatever you want."

Winnie's dimples flashed. "Now I can have revenge. Hooray!" Then she held out the plastic sandwich bag

Elly had used to protect her note. "Now, tell me what this is?"

"Why—it's a sandwich bag," Elly said.

"But what is this substance?" Winnie rubbed the bag between her fingers.

"Plastic! Don't you know what plastic is?" Elly was astonished. "How do you take your lunch to school? Or—I bet you buy your lunch."

Winnie looked confused. "Lunch? Do you mean dinner? We come home for dinner."

"I mean the meal you eat at noon. Is that dinner?"

"Of course, that's dinner."

This was amazing. She and Winnie didn't even use the same words for things. And Winnie didn't know about plastic!

"Winnie, we use plastic for everything." Elly paused. "Although, of course, we're worried about our landfills, but still we have plastic bags and plastic plates and cups and silverware . . ."

"Silverware isn't silver anymore?" Winnie broke in.

Elly laughed. "I mean, forks and spoons and stuff. And oh, what else is different? Computers! We have computers! Have you heard of them?"

Winnie shook her head.

"You don't have television yet, do you? Or VCRs?"

Winnie continued to shake her head, looking awestruck.

"Have you ever heard of cars?" Elly asked. "Automobiles?"

"Oh, yes," Winnie said. "I've heard of automobiles. I've even ridden in one."

"In my time," Elly said eagerly, "almost everyone has a car. Some people even have two!"

"Two automobiles?" Winnie said, astonished.

"Oh, Winnie!" Elly grabbed Winnie's hand. "Won't this be fun!"

"Who's the president?" Winnie asked. "Do you still have presidents?"

"Of course! Who's yours?"

"Mr. Taft."

"My mother says that one of these days we'll have a woman president."

Winnie blinked. "How can that be? Men will never vote for a woman, and women can't vote."

"Women can't vote!" Elly repeated, shocked. "Oh, Winnie, you would love my time. Women can do anything! There are women astronauts and women pilots and women bankers and women—anything!"

She took a deep breath. "Winnie, do you want to come into my time? Do you want to try the locket?"

Winnie's eyes gleamed. "Yes!"

Elly grabbed Winnie's hand. "Come on, let's go."

They crawled out of the hideout and stood up, gazing at each other with excited eyes. Then Winnie frowned.

"Something has just occurred to me. What if I can't get back to my own time?"

Elly hadn't thought of that. What if *she* got stuck in 1912?

But that hadn't happened. "The locket always works," she said. "I always get back to my own time."

"One more question," Winnie said. "Does it hurt? I'm not afraid," she added quickly. "I just want to know."

"You'll get a little dizzy," Elly said, trying to sound reassuring. "That's all."

"Okay, as you say." Winnie held out her hand. "Let's try it."

10

1912

But nothing worked. When Elly removed the locket to give to Winnie, she returned to her own time—with the locket.

When they held hands as Elly unfastened the locket, she returned to her own time, alone. And when Winnie slipped her hand inside the chain as Elly unfastened the locket, the same thing happened. Nothing worked.

"Too bad," Winnie said.

Elly nodded, disappointed. "I wanted to show you the future."

"Or both of us could have seen the past."

Elly caught her breath. "I didn't think of that," she said. "We could have gone to ancient Egypt and watched the pyramids being built ..."

"Or the Revolutionary War," Winnie said. "We could have met George Washington!"

"Or Cleopatra!"

"Or William Shakespeare!"

Elly put her hand over her heart and sighed deeply. " 'O Romeo, Romeo! wherefore art thou Romeo?' "

Winnie giggled. " 'Oh Juliet, parting is such sweet sorrow.' "

Then Elly sighed. "I guess this is it. You and me here, in nineteen twelve. Darn."

Winnie clicked her tongue and looked slyly at Elly. "That's swearing."

Elly almost laughed. "Darn?" Swearing? If Winnie thought "darn" was a swear word, she'd be shocked to hear the kids at Elly's school.

"Anyway," Winnie added, "there's plenty to do right here. For one thing, we can swing. Let's go!"

Elly froze. She'd forgotten about the swing.

Winnie hurried up the slope as Elly stood, motionless, on the path. Then Winnie turned and called, "Come on, Elly!"

Elly followed slowly. She could not get on that rope.

At the top of the path, Winnie said, "What's the matter? Don't you want to swing?"

Elly studied Winnie's face. Could she tell her the truth? Would Winnie laugh at her? Would she still want to be friends?

Elly couldn't take the chance. "Let's explore, instead," she suggested.

Winnie's face fell. "Oh Elly, it's like flying! Please?"

Elly clutched her cast. "I can't. I'm sorry." She tried to make her voice sound regretful. "Do you want me to watch while you swing?"

Winnie smiled. "No, that's no fun for you. We'll explore. But some day will you swing with me?"

Some day? That was easy. Elly would be over this stupid fear any day now. "Sure."

Winnie grinned. "Good. Let's go!" She led the way back down the path to the bottom, and Elly followed, full of relief. She hadn't had to swing, and Winnie still liked her.

They spent hours exploring the ravine that day and the next day and every day after that. Elly was careful to keep her gaze on her feet when she was at the top of the ravine and to avoid places that gave her that fainting feeling of falling.

She was also careful to put on her locket only when she was outside and out of Grandma's sight. She didn't know what happened when she went back to 1912. Did she disappear? She didn't want to frighten her grandmother.

One thing she did know: Grandma would have no reason to worry when Elly was in the ravine for hours. The kitchen clock on the Fourth of July had shown her that time stopped when she went back to the past. No matter how long she was gone, as far as Grandma was concerned she hadn't been gone at all.

Every day, Elly and Winnie followed new trails and discovered secret corners made by bushes and rocks. They found new wildflowers for their Impression Albums and slippery stones that had been smoothed by the little stream. They found a small hollowed-out area in the bank of the ravine that was like a little cave and a pile of stones they decided must mark a burial spot.

"Could be an animal's grave," Winnie said in a low voice, "or even an Indian's."

"You mean Native American," Elly corrected. She

giggled at Winnie's puzzled expression and then explained.

One day they came again upon the pile of old boards and rocks at the base of the Schuyler Street bridge. But this time they heard voices.

Winnie pulled Elly back behind a tree. "I was right," she whispered. "That is my brothers' fort. I recognize their voices."

"What are they saying?" Elly asked. She strained her ears, but she couldn't make out the words.

Winnie shook her head. "I can't tell. Go over there and listen."

Elly grinned. "That's right. They can't see me."

They couldn't hear her either, but Elly couldn't help tiptoeing along the path to the entrance of their fort.

"Diamonds!" said a voice triumphantly, and Elly's heart jumped. Were they talking about jewels?

But one voice groaned and another said, "Three," and there was a slap, slap, slap sound, and Elly groaned herself as she realized what the boys were doing.

She reported back to Winnie. "They're playing cards," she said in a disgusted tone.

"Oh, well," Winnie said and her dimples flashed. "Now we know where they are. We can spy on them whenever we want." She headed upstream. "Come on. I'm hungry. Maybe Rosie'll give us something to eat."

When they got to Grandma's back yard, Elly didn't think twice. She followed Winnie up the steps and into the house, and then she jerked to a halt.

She was back in the same strange kitchen she had seen weeks ago. "Winnie," she breathed. "Is this your house?"

Winnie made a face at her. "Of course it is, silly."

Elly stood still, staring at everything. She and Winnie had spent all their time together outside, in the garden, in the ravine, or in the carriage house. She had shoved all thoughts of this strange place out of her mind.

Now here she was again, and she could see that despite the huge black stove, and the old-fashioned sink, and the scrubbed pine table, this was the same room as Grandma's kitchen. The windows were in the same places, the walls were in the same places, and even the sink, although it was funny-looking, was on the same wall.

There was no one else in the room. Elly turned to Winnie. "Will you show me the rest of the house?"

Winnie nodded. "All right." Her dimples flashed. "But don't say anything. I'd have to answer, and then my family would wonder who I was talking to."

Elly grinned and ran her finger over her lips as if she were zipping them shut. Then, as she followed Winnie out of the kitchen, she wondered if zippers had existed in 1912.

Standing in the front hall, she could hardly believe this was Grandma's house. Oriental carpets covered the floor, tables full of potted plants were jammed into corners, and heavy draperies with tassels and cords hung at the windows. "It's all so fancy," she whispered.

"Shh!" Winnie grinned at her.

Elly clapped a hand over her mouth, but she stared at everything. The wallpaper was ugly—huge, dark red flowers—and so was the purplish carpet on the stairs.

Upstairs, Winnie stopped at the door to the back corner bedroom, and a shiver slid down Elly's spine. Winnie glanced around, then spoke into Elly's ear. "This room belongs to me and my sister." And she opened the door to Elly's room.

Elly tiptoed in, looking at everything, as Winnie closed the door behind them. There were still two windows, but the curtains were made of lace, not plain white cotton. Wallpaper still covered the walls, but the flowers were pink, not yellow, and instead of two twin beds jutting out from the side wall, there was only one big one.

"Winnie," she said softly, "in my time, this is my room."

Winnie looked puzzled. "Your room?"

"You know, the room I stay in when I visit my grandmother."

"I didn't know this was your grandmother's house!"

Elly smiled. "Of course it is, silly," she said, repeating Winnie's earlier words. "Why else am I always here?"

"But that is wonderful!" Winnie's dimples peeked at Elly. "You can tell me all about it in your time!"

But Elly's eye had been caught by a doll sitting on a dresser top. She had a china face, long curling blonde hair, and a dark red dress trimmed with lace. "Oh, Winnie, is she yours?"

Winnie nodded proudly and handed the doll to Elly to hold. "Her name is Charlotte."

"She's beautiful," Elly breathed, fingering the lace on the collar.

Winnie squatted and opened the bottom drawer of the dresser. Another doll, this one with a blue dress instead of a red one and brown hair instead of blonde, lay in the drawer. "This is my sister's. She never plays with her any more."

Elly knelt and wrapped a brown ringlet around her finger. "She's beautiful, too," she said.

"Her name is Harriet," Winnie said. "Maybe some time I could bring both of them outside, and we could play dolls."

"That would be wonderful." Elly hadn't played dolls in a long time, but she had always wanted an old-fashioned doll with a china face and fancy clothes.

Winnie closed the drawer and then put her own doll back on the dresser top. "Come on, let's go get some cookies." She headed for the door. Elly took a final look at the room, then followed Winnie slowly down the stairs, staring again at everything.

Outside, they sat on the stone bench, munching sugar cookies. Elly gazed at the back of Grandma's house. "That was fun," she said.

Winnie nodded. "Next time, I'll show you the secret drawer in my desk."

Elly drew in her breath. A secret drawer. "You are so lucky," she said to Winnie.

Winnie gave a little laugh. "To be truthful, it's not exactly a secret drawer, just extra space underneath one of the little top drawers. But I can hide things there from my brothers and my sister."

"Wow." Elly grinned with delight. There were so many things to see! "Let's go downtown sometime," she said. "And to the college, and . . ." Where else had her grandparents taken her? "I want to see the whole city!"

"We'll take the trolley," Winnie said. "I'll show you my school, and the Erie Canal, and the library . . . and everything!"

She grinned at Elly and Elly grinned back. She hadn't

known there were libraries back in 1912. But they couldn't have had very many books. Think of all the books that had been written since 1912!

"You've got sugar on your lip." Winnie giggled. "It looks like a white mustache." She paused. "I wonder if you'll still be hungry when you get back to your own time?"

"Good question," Elly said, licking the sugar from her lip. Then she jumped up. "But I'm not now. Let's go back to the ravine."

Later, when it was time to go inside, Winnie grabbed Elly's hand as they emerged from the bushes. "I've got an idea," she said, and whispered in her ear.

Elly giggled. "Okay."

Together they crossed the grass and climbed the back steps.

They grinned at each other. "Ready?" Winnie whispered.

Elly nodded. "Set, Go!"

They gave each other little waves, and then together they walked into the house as Elly unfastened her locket.

She giggled as she shook off her dizziness and then looked around the kitchen. Across the years, Winnie was standing in the same spot!

"Hi, Elly. What's so funny?" Grandma turned from the sink and smiled.

Elly gave her a one-armed hug. "I'm just happy, Grandma."

Grandma hugged back. "So am I, Elly. I'm glad you're here."

"Me too," Elly said.

That night as she was getting ready for bed, she remembered Winnie's secret drawer. She wandered across the room to her own desk, pulled down the top, and inspected the little drawers. It would be great to have her own secret place.

But all the drawers seemed to fit snugly. The one in the middle where she'd found the locket had a little extra room—which was probably how the locket and the stamps had gotten stuck—but it wouldn't hold more than the tiniest of secrets.

11

Spying

The days rolled by. Elly went to the ballet twice with Grandma. She played Scrabble with Grandpa. She visited Gee Gee. She baked pies and read books and added names and dates to the family tree, and one day she snipped tiny photographs of Mom and Dad small enough to fit into her locket.

Every day she played with Winnie. Some days they worked in the garden. One of the flowerbeds along the side of the house belonged to Winnie. She had planted pansies there and Sweet William and some red flowers she called pinks. She gave Elly a lesson in weeding.

Some days they played in the carriage house, climbing on the buggy and brushing the horses, and some days Winnie was allowed to take her doll and her sister's doll outside.

Winnie didn't ask Elly to swing again. Maybe it was because Elly still had the cast on her arm. Maybe it was because Elly never mentioned the swing herself. Whatever the reason, Elly was grateful. She didn't want to lie to Winnie, but she knew she wasn't ready to get on that rope.

Almost every day Rosie, the hired girl, gave Winnie cookies or fruit or pieces of cake for little picnics.

"Doesn't she ever ask why you want so much food?" Elly asked, happily eyeing the huge slices of chocolate cake Winnie had just brought into the hideout.

Winnie shook her head. "She thinks all children need to eat all the time."

Elly grinned. "And she's right."

They chewed silently for a while, then Winnie asked, "What's your favorite food?"

"Pizza. What's yours?"

Winnie held up the cake in her hand. "Chocolate cake. What's pizza?"

Winnie didn't know what pizza was! Elly tried to explain, then said, "I'll bring you a piece some day. How about hamburgers? Do you know what they are? Or hot dogs?"

Winnie made a horrified face. "Do you eat dog meat?"

Elly laughed and explained.

"Oh, frankfurters," Winnie said. "I've heard of them."

Something else they did almost every day was spy on the boys. They eavesdropped at the fort under the bridge, they hid behind the carriage house when the boys were playing inside, and they trailed them through the ravine, down one path, over another.

One day Elly was listening outside the boys' fort when she heard them talking about a new house. "I didn't catch it all," she told Winnie as they went back up the ravine. "You're not moving to a new house, are you?"

Winnie shook her head. "I wonder . . ." She frowned. "There's a house being built a few doors down, but Papa strictly forbade our playing in it. I wonder if that's what they're talking about."

They sat down on the stone bench in the garden and spread out some new leaves they had gathered.

"What's this one?" Elly pointed to a leaf with jagged edges and red veins.

"Hmmm." Winnie was peering at the leaf when the boys crashed out of the bushes and thundered past.

Instinctively, Elly shrank back, but Winnie called out, "Where are you going?"

"Nowhere!" one of the big boys yelled. The youngest one turned and stuck out his tongue.

They vanished into the bushes at the side of the house.

"Come on." Winnie pulled Elly to her feet. "Let's follow them."

They ran across the grass to a path through the bushes. "Where do you think they're going?" Elly asked.

"Shhh! They may be playing a trick on me." Winnie crept along the path and Elly followed, through the bushes and into the yard of the house next door. The boys were not there.

But voices sounded somewhere ahead. Elly looked questioningly at Winnie, and Winnie nodded. "That's them," she whispered. "Let's see what they're up to."

They slipped from that backyard to the next, creeping from bush to house corner to bush, following the voices.

Elly had forgotten how new everything had looked

the other time she'd ventured into Winnie's neighborhood. Now she ran alongside Winnie, staring at everything, trying not to trip, and thinking, 1912! This is all 1912!

Porches were sturdy, paint was shiny, and windows shone. And the trees! A few were as tall as the houses, but most of them looked as if they'd just been planted. The big oaks of Grandma's neighborhood were only babies now. Elly giggled at the thought.

"Shh!" Winnie hissed, then giggled herself. "I know they can't hear you, but you'll make me talk and they'll hear *me!*"

Elly grinned, and Winnie grabbed her hand. "Come on!" she said. They crept along some bushes bordering one yard and moved quietly into the next. A woman wearing a long dress was hanging wet clothes on a line, and some little girls wearing black tights like Winnie's were playing dolls on the back steps.

"Hello, Winnie," the woman said, and the little girls waved.

Elly held her breath. Was she invisible to them as well as to Winnie's brothers? Just in case, she smiled politely, hoping her T-shirt and shorts wouldn't shock them if they could see her.

"Hello, Mrs. Abernathy," Winnie said. "Did you see my brothers go this way?"

"I saw Howie!" one of the little girls called. "He went into the vacant lot, and so did the big boys."

"Thanks, Gladys," Winnie said.

"Is something wrong with your arm, dear?" the woman asked, pointing to Winnie's hand, the one that held Elly's. "You're holding it so stiffly."

She didn't see Elly! Elly fought back a giggle as

Winnie quickly raised and lowered the arm. "No, it's fine, thank you, Mrs. Abernathy. 'Bye!" Winnie waved and pulled Elly through the bushes into the vacant lot beyond.

Safe on the other side, they looked at each other and burst into giggles, smothering them with their hands. "Is something wrong with your arm, Winnie?" Elly quoted the woman.

Winnie giggled, moving the arm up and down. "It's so stiff," she said, and fresh giggles burst out of them.

"Come on," Winnie said at last. "Let's find the boys. I bet they've gone to the new house."

They crossed the vacant lot, and there, beyond the bushes, was a large, cleared area. A partially-built house rose from the dirt.

Winnie put her finger to her lips. She spoke into Elly's ear. "A rich banker's building this house, but no one's working on it now. People say he's lost his money and can't afford it anymore."

The walls were up, but the windows were only holes and there was no door in the doorway. Elly could hear faint shouts, and then two figures appeared in one of the windows.

"My brothers," Winnie whispered. "Papa would tan their hides if he found out. You go around that side. I'll take this one. Let's see what they're doing."

They separated, Winnie moving softly along the back of the property and Elly sticking to the shrubs of the neighboring lot until she was close to the side walls of the new house.

"I'm king!" a voice shouted. "King of the mountain!"

Through the empty windows, Elly could see one of

the boys standing in the upstairs hall, his arms flung wide. The passageway was without a railing guarding it from the floor below.

She froze.

"I'm king!" the boy shouted again. He leaned forward.

"Hey, Eddie, James!" he shouted. "I'm king—" He lost his balance and pitched forward, his arms flailing, and Elly heard a long scream.

She stood, unmoving, hearing the scream over and over.

"Elly!" Winnie called. "Help!" She was climbing into the hole of the open door.

The air was full of screams.

"Elly!" Winnie cried.

12

A Phone Call

The scream continued, over and over and over, as memories of the accident in Maine washed over Elly.

Mom—

"Help!" Winnie cried.

"Howie! Get up!" one of the boys yelled.

Figures were scurrying around inside the house. "Stop that!" Winnie shouted. "We can't move him yet! Someone go get Mother."

One of the boys went jumping out of the open doorway, and the others all knelt beside Howie. The screams stopped, and only Winnie's quiet voice could be heard.

"It's all right, Howie," she said. "It's all right. Let's find something to cover him."

The older boys took off their shirts and Winnie draped them lightly over her little brother.

That was to keep him from going into shock, Elly knew. That was what the teacher-friends had done for her mother.

Mom—

Elly sank onto the grass, her knees shaking, seeing Howie fall, over and over—

"Mama!"

Elly's eyes jerked open. A pretty woman with a long skirt had climbed into the house, along with one of Winnie's brothers and a man carrying a black bag.

Elly closed her eyes with a moan. She'd thought she was better. She still had nightmares, but she could go back to sleep on her own. She could watch Winnie swing without running into the house. She could play in the ravine for hours without thinking about falling or about Mom . . .

Mom. Elly took a shuddering breath. Now she knew she was as full of fear as when she had first come to Grandma's. Nothing had changed. Nothing.

After a long time, after Winnie's little brother had been carried away and Winnie and the others had all gone, Elly slowly unfastened the locket where she still sat on the grass.

The locket fell into her hands. Dizziness swirled around her, and something poked at her face.

She was sitting in a tangle of shrubbery. The house that had been half-built in 1912 had been finished for a long time. It rose in front of her, shabby, needing a coat of paint, its porches sagging.

Elly pushed her way out of the bushes and headed slowly for home. Everything seemed in need of repair these days.

"You're not wearing the locket," Gee Gee said.

Elly looked up with a start. She'd been gazing out

the nursing home window, her mind a jumble of worries and fears.

"Sorry?" she said to Gee Gee.

"You're not wearing the locket."

"No." Elly rubbed the spot on her T-shirt where the little heart lay when she wore the locket.

"So, where is it?" Gee Gee asked, and something in her voice made Elly look sharply at the old woman. Gee Gee had acted so weird the day Elly had asked about the locket that she was surprised she'd remembered anything about the visit.

"Here." Elly pulled the necklace from her shorts' pocket and displayed it on the palm of her hand.

Gee Gee snatched it away and peered at it. Elly drew in her breath. Would she give it back? It was hard to know what this strange Gee Gee would do.

Grandma patted Elly's hand as if to say "Humor Gee Gee for now." She turned to Gee Gee. "Do you recognize the locket, Mama? Was it yours?"

"Yes," Gee Gee said shortly.

Elly watched the old gnarled fingers curl around the little heart, and she felt numb with anxiety. Without the locket, she would never see Winnie again—if Winnie would want to see her after what had happened at the empty house.

Gee Gee pried open the little heart, squinted at the tiny photographs of Elly's parents, then clicked it shut. "Here," she said, and handed the locket back to Elly. "This is yours now."

Elly closed her eyes with relief. She slipped the necklace into her pocket and kept her hand tight around it.

*   *   *

That night as she was clearing the table after dinner, the telephone rang. It was Uncle Don.

"Oh, too bad," Grandma said at first into the receiver. Then—"No, that would be wonderful! Elly will be thrilled. Let Kate tell her."

Puzzled, Elly took the phone, and then her cousin Kate was blaring at her. "Elly! I'm coming tomorrow! I'm not going camping with Jessica after all!"

Shock made Elly speechless.

"Jessica has *chicken pox*—can you believe it?—and so does her little brother. So they're not going camping, and Mom and Dad said I can come to Grandma's instead—tomorrow!"

Elly dropped into a chair.

"Won't it be great? I can't wait to see what you've done on the fort! We can start the second story!"

"Yeah." Elly swallowed. "Great."

At last Kate finished chattering and Elly could hang up the phone and go upstairs to her room. Kate—coming tomorrow.

She wasn't ready for Kate to come. She was still having nightmares. She was still terrified of falling. She was still—chicken.

Elly looked across at the other twin bed. That's what Kate would call her. Chicken. She wouldn't be able to climb into the fort, let alone work on it, and how could she get away to be with Winnie? Assuming Winnie would even want to be with her after this afternoon.

Elly crept under her covers. If only Mom were here. If only she could talk to Mom.

If only the whole horrible accident had never happened and she and Mom could be the way they used to be.

If only—if only she hadn't stood by so stupidly as her mother fell and fell and fell . . .

Elly picked up the locket lying on her nightstand and rubbed the little heart until it grew warm in her hand. She lay for a long time, holding the locket and remembering Gee Gee's old fingers doing the same thing that afternoon.

13

Cousin Kate

The next morning Grandma was full of plans for Kate's visit. "We'll go to the ballet on Thursday," she said at breakfast, scribbling a list. "And on Sunday, how about the State Museum?"

Elly's heart sank. Not only would Kate want to work on the fort and take her time away from Winnie, Grandma would have a million things for them to do as well.

"Maybe one day we'll go to the dollhouse store," Grandma was saying, "and . . . oh, dear. We can't go swimming this year, can we?"

Elly looked down at her cast. "*I* can't. But I wouldn't mind if you took Kate to the pool." That way she could be with Winnie at least one day.

"Silly!" Grandma shook her head. "We can't go without you! But I'm sure we'll find plenty to do. Maybe Kate would like to help on the family tree."

Elly escaped outside as soon as she could after breakfast, praying she'd be able to find Winnie. She sat down on the stone bench and slipped the locket around her neck.

After the dizziness left her, she saw that the garden was empty. She went into the ravine and searched, but the ravine was empty as well.

Where was Winnie? The only place left to look was her house. Elly cringed at that thought, but she had to find Winnie.

It was creepy, sneaking through Winnie's house without her. Elly felt like a thief. And even though she checked every room of the house, she couldn't find her. Rosie was cooking in the kitchen, the big boys were working in the cellar, and the little brother was lying in his bed with his mother at his side. How badly was he hurt? Elly couldn't tell, and she couldn't find Winnie.

Maybe she was outside by now. Elly checked the garden and the ravine again, but again no one was there.

She sighed, discouraged, as she trudged back up the path. Her time with Winnie was running out.

Back at the top of the ravine, she slipped off her necklace, waited for the dizziness to pass, and then, down the path, she caught sight of the fort she and Kate had built. She paused.

If she could do it now, by herself, before Kate arrived . . . no one was here to watch . . .

At the fort tree, the boards nailed into the trunk waited in front of her. She reached for one, then looked up at the platform, high overhead.

She'd keep her gaze on her feet as she climbed. Then, up there, she'd look straight across, not down . . . make her mind go numb . . . she could do it . . .

But what if she slipped on one of the steps? What if she slipped on the platform and fell, over the edge—

The rocks—

She shuddered and turned away. She was still afraid.
Still chicken.

For the rest of the day, Grandma kept Elly busy. They
made two pies—blueberry this time. They cleared out
drawers in Elly's dresser. They put fresh sheets on
Kate's bed. They went to the grocery store and came
home with eight bags of groceries.

"That ought to feed two growing girls for a few
days," Grandma said as they put the food away.

Darkness was blurring the bushes by the time Kate
arrived with her family. She bounded out of the car.
"Elly! Let's go! Let's go to the fort!"

Elly sighed, but Grandma came to her rescue. "Abso-
lutely not," Grandma said. "It's too dark to play in
the ravine."

"But Grandma," Kate wailed. "We have to see our
fort. We'll be careful."

But Grandma shook her head firmly. "Your fort will
wait until tomorrow," she said.

A reprieve, Elly thought thankfully as she followed
Kate upstairs to their room.

"I can't believe it!" Kate burst out after she'd closed
their door. "After all this time, I have to wait even
longer."

"Too bad," Elly said, pretending to be sympathetic.
"Want to play cards?"

They played gin rummy until bedtime, and it felt like
every other summer vacation with Kate.

But, just as Elly had feared, nightmares jerked her
awake, moaning, in the middle of the night.

Kate was standing over her. "What's the matter, Elly? Bad dream?"

Elly just nodded, her heart thudding, praying Kate wouldn't make fun of her.

"Think about your favorite movie," Kate said. "Every single scene. That's what I do. It'll make the nightmare go away and help you go back to sleep."

"Okay," Elly said, relieved. Someone must have warned Kate about the nightmares. Elly hated the thought that her family was talking about her, but she was glad not to be teased.

Breakfast the next morning was a leisurely meal. Grandma had made blueberry pancakes, and Elly and Kate and Kate's brother, Robbie, ate one after another as the grownups talked and drank coffee.

At last, Kate's family left for their home in Syracuse, but Elly and Kate had to help with the dishes. After the plates and bowls and coffee cups were in the dishwasher, Grandma announced that it was time to work on the Eleanor Tree.

Kate was interested in that, to Elly's surprise. "After all, my middle name is Eleanor," Kate said. She added her own name and her brother's and her parents', and Grandma let her put Gee Gee's name in the proper spot. "Eleanor Louise Hamilton," Kate printed neatly.

And then it was lunchtime and Grandma told them she'd planned a trip to the miniatures store. "I think it's time your dollhouses had some new furniture, don't you?" Neither Kate nor Elly could resist that invitation.

By the time they returned home—Elly with a tiny grand piano for her dollhouse parlor, and Kate with a little rocking horse for her nursery—it was late afternoon.

91

Elly and Kate put away their purchases in their bedroom. "What a great day!" Kate said. "And the best part is still ahead." She grabbed Elly's hand. "Let's go, Elly! Tree fort, here we come!"

There were no more delays. Elly trudged after Kate down the stairs and outside to the garden. Kate plunged into the honeysuckle bushes, and Elly slowly followed.

"At last!" Kate said when they came out onto the path. "I can't wait to see what you've done!"

Elly's heart sank. "Well . . ." She trailed after Kate as she marched down the path toward the fort. "I haven't . . ."

Kate scrambled up the supports they'd nailed into the tree trunk, then Elly heard her disbelieving voice. "It looks the same!"

Kate hung over the platform, an incredulous look on her face. "You haven't touched it!"

"I—I know. My arm . . ." Elly clutched her cast. "It's hard to do anything with this."

Kate stared. "But you didn't even clean it up. It's a mess! Leaves all over the place, and dirt, and squirrels have been up here, and . . ."

She climbed back down the tree. "I'm going to get a broom and clean this up—" She stopped to give Elly a disapproving look. "You're going to help now, aren't you?"

Elly forced herself to look up at the platform of the fort, and then out across the ravine. Her stomach dropped.

"I don't know . . ."

"Elly! It's not fair to make me do all the work." Kate frowned. "You can get up there with your cast. I've had a broken arm before. I know you can do it."

"I—I . . ." What could Elly say? *I'm afraid of things like windows and stairs and forts? I've become a baby about heights? I'm chicken?*

"I just can't," she said finally and turned away.

"What's the matter with you, Elly?" Kate said. "Where are you going? Why won't you help?"

Elly plodded down the path. She didn't know what to say to Kate.

"Great!" came Kate's voice. Her tone was sarcastic. "Just great. This is going to be a fun week."

14

Grandma's Book

Kate was right. It was going to be a horrible week. Elly trudged down the path until she was past the curve.

She glanced behind her. No sign of Kate. She pulled the locket from her shorts. She'd go find Winnie, and they'd play in the hideout, protected, safe . . .

If Winnie would want to be with her after what had happened at the empty house.

Elly sighed. She slipped the locket around her neck and, as soon as the dizziness left her, moved cautiously down the path to the bottom of the ravine.

Winnie poked her head from the hideout's entrance. "Elly! I thought I heard you coming. Where have you been?"

Winnie wasn't mad. Elly smiled in relief.

"I have the best news," Winnie said. "Come in and I'll tell you all about it."

Elly scrambled into the hideout after her. "How's your brother? Was he badly hurt? I'm sorry I couldn't—"

Winnie smiled. "He's fine. Only a broken leg." She

paused, her expression suddenly glum. "But we all got in trouble. I had to weed all the flower gardens, front and back. Papa said we must not have enough to do if we have time to poke around other people's houses."

"Oh, no," Elly said. Winnie must have been in the front garden when Elly was searching for her.

Winnie brightened. "But that's over, and I have my good news. Two pieces of good news. First," she said, "I may be getting a locket for my birthday. I overheard my aunt talking to my mother about giving me one."

"Maybe it'll be magic like mine!" Elly said. "Maybe you'll be able to come into *my* time!"

Winnie's dimples flashed. "That would be wonderful!"

"We'll have so much fun!" Elly grinned with delight. "I'll show you television and movies and—" She paused at a sudden thought. "Keep it in that secret place you told me about, remember? In your desk?" Elly tried to remember Winnie's desk from the times she'd been in Winnie's room. Wouldn't it be weird if it turned out to be her desk? The house and the furniture must have been sold many times since 1912, but . . .

Suddenly, Elly was electrified. What if Winnie did keep her locket in that desk, and then, eighty years later, Elly found a locket in her own desk? If they were the same desk, would it be the same locket?

"Don't you want to know my second piece of good news?"

With difficulty, Elly pulled her thoughts from the locket. "Sure."

Winnie's smile split her face. "My friend Olivia, the one who was quarantined, is past the danger point! She's going to be all right. Her sister came over today to tell me."

"Oh Winnie, I'm really glad," Elly said.

"Me too," Winnie said. "I've been so worried. Ever since Helen—died, I . . ." Her voice trailed away, and Elly saw a hint of the sadness that had filled her face when they had first met. "But now, she'll be able to come outside soon, and we can all play together." She grinned. "Us against the boys."

Elly frowned. "But she won't be able to see me."

Winnie's face fell. "I forgot."

"And you'd better not *tell* her about me either," Elly said, wondering what Kate would say if she told her. "She'll think you're nuts."

Winnie giggled. "Nuts?"

"Crazy," Elly said. "Loony."

Winnie grinned, then jumped up. "Come on! Let's go spy on the boys. *They're* the ones who are nuts."

Then Elly and Winnie scrambled out of the hideout and headed down the ravine, and everything felt right. Elly marched happily along the path. She wouldn't give Kate or the fort another thought.

But then Winnie jerked to a halt and grabbed Elly's good arm. "Let's swing instead!" she said. "Your arm is better, and the rope is so much fun!"

All Elly's good feelings fled. She looked up at the tree that held the rope swing, up, up, up, and she was silent.

"You promised," Winnie said. "Remember? You said 'some day' you'd swing with me."

"I remember." But Elly hadn't known her stupid fears would last so long.

"Please?" Winnie said. "Soon Olivia will be able to swing, and we can have such fun together." Her dimples flashed. "Even if she can't see you."

96

A sudden picture of Winnie and her friend swinging across the ravine away from her sprang into Elly's mind. "I'll try," she said.

"Oh, goody!" Winnie pulled Elly up the ravine. "I know you can do it, Elly," she bubbled. "You're so brave, traveling through time. I know you can swing on a rope."

But Elly looked back up at the tree and said nothing. Silently, she followed Winnie up the path to the top of the ravine. Winnie slid the rope from its branch and narrowed her eyes thoughtfully at Elly. "Now, let's see . . ."

Elly tried to block out thought. If she didn't think about how high she would be over the ravine, if she didn't think about the rocks—or Mom . . .

"Up you go." Winnie boosted her up onto the knot of the rope. "Grab on tight. I'll get us going and then I'll jump up there with you. Ready?"

Elly grabbed onto the rope with one hand, and the rope swayed with her weight.

"Ready," she said.

Walking backward, Winnie pulled them away from the ravine, back, back . . .

Elly's stomach dropped.

She closed her eyes, but that was worse. She felt herself falling—

"No," she whispered.

"Elly, you can do it," Winnie said.

What if the weight of two girls was too much and the rope didn't make it all the way back? They'd be stranded, dangling over the rocks . . .

"Please, Elly," Winnie said.

What if the extra weight made the rope break? They'd fall, crashing onto the rocks . . .

"No!" Elly said. "Stop!"

Winnie sighed. "All right. You don't have to make a fuss."

"I'm sorry, Winnie," Elly said miserably. "I just can't."

"Oh well," Winnie said, and Elly watched her eye the rope and then look out across the ravine. She knew Winnie wanted to swing, and she thought again of her with her friend, swinging out over the ravine, leaving Elly behind.

Chicken. She *was* chicken.

Grandma and Grandpa had planned to take the girls out to dinner that evening, but as Elly went to her room to change she did not feel festive.

Afraid to climb to the fort. Afraid to swing on the rope. Kate, mad at her. Winnie, disappointed in her . . .

Winnie had promised to meet her after dinner, but would she keep her promise? Would she want to be with a chicken?

Elly and Kate washed and changed and then sat silently in the back seat of the car as Grandpa drove to the restaurant.

"Isn't this fun?" Grandma said brightly as they seated themselves in the dining room. "Isn't this a treat?"

Elly knew she had sensed the coolness between the girls, and she didn't want her to worry. "Great," she said and forced a smile. "Thanks, Grandma. Thanks, Grandpa."

Kate tried to be polite too. "Everything looks good,"

she said, gazing at the menu. "I don't know what to have."

But it was hard to keep up the pretense. After they had chatted about the food and their plans for the week, silence fell on the group. Grandma, seeming to cast about for a conversational topic, suddenly said, "Elly, you're not wearing your locket! It would have looked sweet with that dress."

Before Elly could reply, Grandma turned to Kate and said, "Did Elly show you the locket she found?"

Elly's heart thudded.

"No," Kate said. "She didn't." She gave Elly a questioning look.

Elly tried to sound casual. "It's just an old necklace." If Kate wore the locket, would it take her back to 1912 too? *She* wouldn't be afraid to swing on the rope with Winnie.

Grandpa changed the topic. "What's black and white and red all over?"

"A newspaper?" Kate guessed.

Elly tried to be polite too. "A zebra that fell down the stairs?"

"Nope," Grandpa said. "An embarrassed penguin."

They all laughed, and after Grandpa had told a few more riddles, the meal was over and it was time to go home. Elly glanced at her watch. Soon it would be time to meet Winnie. *If* Winnie still wanted to be with her. Elly leaned her head back against the car seat and sighed.

"Elly, you seem tired," Grandma said when they got home. "I'd thought we could watch a video, but ... Would you rather go to bed?"

It was still light outside. Was Elly such a baby that

she had to go to bed while the sun was shining? "I'm fine, Grandma," she said, and avoided Kate's eye.

"Okay, honey," Grandma said. "Grandpa and I'll watch the news until you and Kate are ready."

Elly wandered upstairs to change out of the dress she'd worn to dinner, but as soon as Kate came in the room Elly grabbed her sneakers and hurried out.

"Elly, wait!" Kate followed her out to the hallway and lowered her voice. "Are you okay? You're acting so weird."

Elly edged away. "I'm all right."

"Well, why won't you work on the fort?" Kate asked. "Why didn't you show me that locket?" Her voice was louder now, angrier. "Where is it?"

Anger mixed with fear and shame blazed up inside Elly. "Just leave me alone, Kate! Leave me *alone*." She whirled and pounded down the stairs and out to the sunroom at the back of the house.

She threw herself into a chair to wait until it was time to meet Winnie. She felt awful. She and Kate never fought. She never would have kept something like the locket from her. She never would have been afraid of a rope swing.

Everything had changed since the accident.

Would she ever be the same again? Would Mom? If only . . .

Furiously, Elly blinked away tears and began tidying up Grandma's stuff for the family tree. Might as well get something done.

Trying not to think, she pulled papers into a pile and tidied the notebooks. She straightened the stack of photographs. The book about the neighborhood had fallen open, and she reached to close it. But two words darted out at her from the page: "rope swing."

She scanned the paragraph and then, with growing horror, read it again: "The significant geological landmark in College Hill is, of course, the ravine that cuts through the neighborhood. Over the years, it has been a playground for neighborhood children, although, sadly, on July 28, 1912, a young girl, Eleanor (Winnie) Hamilton, was killed when a rope swing broke and she plummeted to her death."

There was more, but Elly could read no further. She sat, stunned, her hand covering the page to blot out the words she'd read. But there was no blotting out the thought of Winnie, killed on the rope swing. *Winnie*.

15

The Rope Swing

Elly stared at the words in the book. Winnie, killed in the ravine!

And then the full meaning of the name penetrated her consciousness.

Eleanor Hamilton. Kate had written that name in the Eleanor Tree that afternoon.

Eleanor Hamilton was Gee Gee's name. Gee Gee was Winnie.

Elly's mind whirled, trying to take it all in. Winnie was her great-great-aunt.

She'd thought Winnie's real name must be Winifred or Winona. She'd never heard of "Winnie" being a nickname for Eleanor. She'd never heard that Gee Gee'd had a childhood nickname.

And then she came back to the horror of it: Winnie—*Gee Gee*—killed on the rope swing.

But wait. It made no sense. If Winnie had died, how could she grow up to be Gee Gee? Gee Gee who was an old lady in a nursing home?

"Elly?" It was Kate. "Is something the matter?"

Elly stared at Kate. Could she tell her? It was all so strange. Would Kate believe her? Or would she think that Elly's head injury was making her crazy?

Elly pointed to the words in Grandma's book. "What do you think of this?"

Kate bent over the page and frowned. "Someone died in the ravine? That's awful."

"Doesn't the name look familiar?" Elly asked. "And look at the date—exactly . . . what? Eighty years ago?"

Kate peered at the book. "Not exactly. July twenty-eighth is tomorrow. But the name . . ."

"Tomorrow!" Elly shot up. "It hasn't happened yet! There's time to save her!"

She raced out of the room, barely hearing Kate calling after her.

"Save who? What do you mean? Elly!"

Elly tore out the door, across the grass, and into the ravine, digging in her pocket for the necklace. She'd find Winnie and warn her. There was time. There had to be.

Dizziness swirled over her, and the instant it passed she called, "Winnie!"

No one answered.

"Winnie!"

The ravine was silent.

"WINNIE!" Where was she? They had promised to meet each other here . . .

Elly fled down the path to the bottom of the ravine, grabbing at branches and bushes to keep herself from falling. Was the date wrong? Was she already dead?

There was no body in the ravine. Relief washed over Elly. Winnie was still alive. Winnie was *alive*.

But then she glanced up and saw the rope hanging from its place, waiting.

The horror flooded through her again. She had to find her. Where was she? Elly's gaze darted around the ravine as she tried to think. The hideout?

She raced along the lower path to the hollowed-out bushes. "Winnie!" she called. "Win!" Elly scrambled through the bushes into the center.

No one was there.

She scrambled back out. Where was she? Why didn't she answer? Had she gone into the house?

"Winnie!" Elly screamed. Shadows were gathering in the ravine. Soon it would be dark. Soon it would be tomorrow.

She looked up, way up, at the tree limb holding the rope swing. Was something wrong with the rope? Or was the branch about to break?

No, it must be the rope. A rope, not a branch, had been found at the bottom of the ravine with the body.

She hurried to the path. She would stand guard at the base of the tree. As soon as Winnie arrived, she'd tell her what she'd learned, and she'd be safe.

Winnie would believe her, wouldn't she? She wouldn't think Elly's story was just an excuse so she wouldn't have to swing, would she?

But the minutes passed, and Winnie did not come. No one came.

As Elly waited, her dread grew. There was no one to help her. If she did not find Winnie soon, she knew there was only one thing to do.

She would have to cut down the rope swing. She would have to climb the tree arching high over the ravine and cut down the rope swing.

*   *   *

Elly stood at the base of the tree, her heart pounding. She patted Grandpa's Swiss Army knife, secure in her pocket, as she tried to think calmly about the job ahead.

She looked up at the tree. Plenty of stumpy branches for handholds ... she'd climb up to that branch there ... then over to that one ...

She took a deep breath, slipped her broken arm out of its sling and reached for the first handhold. Don't think about anything, she told herself. Just go.

She swallowed, then pulled herself up, first to one branch, then the second. Her cast banged against the trunk, and the pain made her lose her footing for an instant. Her stomach dropped sickeningly, but she thought, *Winnie—Gee Gee*—and she forced herself to keep going.

When she was high enough, she was able to grab one of the long branches and pull herself up onto it. Don't look down, she told herself. Keep climbing. Think of Winnie. It was like a drumbeat. Win-nie. Win-nie.

At last. There was the knot of the rope, far out on the fourth branch. Her breath caught. Too far out. Winnie's brothers could have killed themselves putting up this swing.

Elly grabbed hold of the branch and sat on it, wrapping her legs around it. She inched forward. Stupid boys. They must have been crazy. Crazy! The anger pushed away a little of the fear.

But only a little. She moved too quickly, and the branch gave a sudden jerk. Her stomach fell like a stone, and she felt herself falling ...

Fear shot though her. Was *she* the girl in the book? Maybe the name was wrong!

Stop, she told herself. Relax. She sat for a moment, breathing deeply, hearing the name in her head: Win-nie. Win-nie.

Then she stretched herself along the branch and pushed forward. Forward to the rope.

The top of the knot looked safe. But then she reached underneath the branch.

Only one strand of the thick rope was still attached to the knot. The other strands had frayed and twisted away.

It would take no weight at all to snap that final strand.

Carefully she shifted slightly on the branch. Carefully she pulled Grandpa's knife from her pocket. Carefully she reached under the branch for the rope—and the branch bounced.

Falling—

Mom—

Winnie.

The name drummed into Elly's head, and she grabbed tight hold of the branch. Winnie. Elly couldn't fall. She had to hold on, for Winnie. For Gee Gee.

She lay stretched along the branch, motionless for a moment, breathing slowly. Nothing she could have done that day in Maine would have prevented an accident. She knew that now. She couldn't have saved her mother from that fall. But today . . . today was another matter.

When she was ready, she reached again for the rope, and this time she didn't let go. She held tight to the rope with her left hand and sawed at it with the knife in her right.

At last the blade cut through that final strand. The rope fell, far down onto the rocks, the knife slipped from her fingers, and then she felt herself falling—

Falling—

16

The Locket

Elly opened her eyes and found she was lying across a huge bush near the bottom of the ravine. What on earth—?

She'd fallen from a giant tree, but she didn't feel hurt. She lay still for a moment, assessing herself. No, no injuries. How weird. A fall like that could have killed her.

But the fall had been weird, too. It hadn't felt like falling exactly, more like . . . what? Floating? Sleeping?

She shook her head and struggled off the bush, branches scratching her legs and arms and catching in her hair.

Why had she fallen, anyway? She'd had a good grip on the tree limb. She hadn't slipped. She had held on tight.

She looked up at the branch that had held the rope swing.

The tree was gone.

She stared. The tree with the huge limb arching over

the ravine, the tree that had supported the rope swing, was gone.

How could that be? Unless—oh no! But the locket was still around her neck.

"Elly!" It was Kate, flying down the path. "Elly! Elly! Elly! Are you all right?"

Elly nodded. "I'm okay."

"I thought I saw you fall." Kate was breathless. "I thought you were dead. Are you sure you're all right?"

Wait a minute. What was Kate doing here? She wasn't from the time of the locket.

Uneasiness crept over Elly. Was something wrong with the locket?

Winnie.

"Come on, Elly," Kate said. "You should go back to the house. You're all scratched up. Is your arm okay?"

Elly struggled to put her attention on Kate. "Yeah, it's fine. Thanks."

She had to know about the locket. "Wait a minute," she said to Kate and unfastened the locket.

There was no dizziness. Her head was steady.

Oh, no . . . She fastened the locket again. Again her head was fine, and again Kate was still beside her.

Something *was* wrong with the locket.

Elly pulled it off and stared at it. She inspected the clasp. Fine. The chain. Fine. The little heart. Fine.

Everything was fine. So why wouldn't the locket work? Why wouldn't it take her back to 1912? Why wouldn't it take her back to Winnie?

"Is that the necklace you found?" Kate was asking. "Can I see it?"

The locket didn't work. How would she ever see Winnie again? *Would* she ever see Winnie again?

"Elly? Can I? Can I see it?"

Oh, Winnie. Elly felt like crying.

"Elly! What's the matter with you? Are you okay?" Kate was studying her face.

Elly tried to focus on Kate. "I guess so." Physically, she was fine.

Kate peered at the locket in Elly's hand. "Can I try it on?"

Elly rubbed the little heart for a moment, then handed the locket to Kate. It didn't seem to matter now who wore it. The magic was gone.

Elly told Kate everything about the locket and Winnie, everything she understood. She had to tell someone, and Kate was the most likely to believe her.

"And then I cut down the rope," Elly finished as they sat together on the stone bench, "and even though I was holding tightly to that branch, I fell." She looked sideways at Kate. "It was weird."

"Weird! I would have been scared to death!" Kate was looking at her with respect. "You are really brave, Elly."

Brave? Elly shook her head. She'd been terrified.

"Let's go look at that book," Kate said. "I want to see something."

Elly's heart sank. Kate didn't believe her. "I'm not making this up," she said.

Kate turned to stare at her. "I know that! I saw what it said in the book before you went out. I know that Gee Gee's name before she got married was Eleanor Hamilton, and I know that she didn't die in nineteen twelve. I just want to check something out."

Relief swept over Elly. Kate did believe her.

"I wish it had happened to me," Kate said. "You lucky duck."

Elly smiled, suddenly. She had been lucky. She had traveled through time. She had met her own great-great-aunt as a girl. "I *was* lucky," she said. But she still wanted the locket to work.

They rose, crossed the lawn, and climbed the back steps to the kitchen door. In the sunroom, they went straight to the table that held all the family tree stuff.

The book was still opened to the passage about the rope swing, and Elly tingled, remembering the shock of reading it the first time. She sank into a chair.

But Kate's words made her sit up straight. "It's gone," Kate said in a whisper, staring at the page. "The part about the rope swing is gone."

"What?" Elly said. She yanked the book across the table and scanned the page for the words "rope swing." Kate was right. The words were gone.

And not only that. The part about the ravine was different. Elly's neck prickled. ". . . Over the years, the ravine has been a playground for neighborhood children, and many adults today have fond memories of playing in 'Dutchman's Hollow.'"

"I don't understand," she said to Kate.

"I guess . . ." Kate hesitated. She sat down in the chair next to Elly. "In a way it makes sense. Winnie—Gee Gee—didn't die. So her death can't be in the book because it never happened." She frowned at Elly. "*Does* it make sense? I remember that time travel book we read last summer . . ."

Elly let Kate ramble as she drew the pages of the Eleanor Tree across the table. "Eleanor Louise Hamil-

110

ton," she read. "Born September 16, 1900." Gee Gee. Winnie.

Grandma poked her head into the sunroom. "Ready to watch a video, girls?"

Elly tried the locket again the next morning, and so did Kate. They tried inside the house and outside. They tried at the top of the ravine and at the bottom of the ravine. They tried everything they could think of, but it was no good. Nothing worked. The magic of the locket was gone.

Elly did find Grandpa's Swiss Army knife lying half-buried in the dirt of the ravine. Dented, rusted, it looked as if it had been there for dozens of years.

In a way, it had been. She had dropped it in the ravine of 1912.

Gently she brushed off the dirt, tears misting her eyes. "I guess I'll have to buy Grandpa a new knife," she said to Kate.

But there was nothing to be done about the locket.

17

Winnie

"I wish the locket still worked," Elly said a few days later to Kate as they sat together in their tree fort. "I don't understand the whole thing."

Kate pounded a nail into the floor. "Me either. Maybe we never will."

Elly nodded. "Or maybe someday, suddenly, the locket will work again. For both of us."

Kate grinned. "Maybe next time, it'll take us forward in time!"

"We could go into outer space!"

"We could go anywhere in the universe!"

"We could meet our own grandchildren!" Elly said, and they burst into laughter. Their conversation reminded Elly of some she'd had with Winnie.

She knew there would be many reminders of Winnie. If Winnie had been in my time, she thought, she would have been my best friend.

"I wish you could have met Winnie," Elly said. "It's weird to think she's Gee Gee."

"I wish Grandma would let us visit her," Kate said. "You could ask her about it."

But Gee Gee had had a bad spell, and although Grandma visited her aunt every day, she wouldn't allow the girls to go. "Remember her as she was," she had said after one of her visits.

"I'll never forget her," Elly had said, and she meant both Gee Gee and the girl Winnie.

She remembered the first day she'd seen Winnie, walking out of the bushes, her face full of sadness. She remembered the mischief in her eyes the foggy morning they'd trailed the boys, and her startled delight when they'd discovered the truth about the locket. By then, Elly realized now, the earlier sadness was gone.

"Hand me a nail, will you, Elly?" Kate held out her hand, and Elly put a nail into it, and they got back to work on the fort.

That night when Grandma called her to the phone, Elly could tell from the smiles wreathing her grandparents' faces that something was up.

But all Grandpa would say was, "Someone wants to talk to you."

Elly put the phone to her ear. "Hello?"

"Hi, honey," said a familiar voice.

"Mom!" Elly said. For the first time, her mother sounded like Mom. "How are you?"

"Terrific," Mom said. "I miss you."

"I miss you, too. When are you getting out of the hospital?"

"It won't be long now. Tell me what you've been doing."

Elly smiled to herself. She couldn't tell her mother

113

what she'd really been doing—traveling through time and saving the life of the girl who would become her great-great-aunt.

"Reading and playing outside with Kate and baking pies with Grandma. Oh, and Mom," she added. "I found a really pretty locket."

"I can't wait to see it," Mom said. "Uh oh. The nurse is here with some disgusting pills, so I have to go. Take care of yourself. I love you, Elly."

"I love you, Mom." Elly hung up the phone and smiled. Things felt all right again.

The next day Kate's parents picked her up and took her home, and that afternoon Elly had the cast taken off her arm.

"Everything getting back to normal, eh, Elly?" Grandpa said at dinner. "Before you know it, your dad'll be bringing your mom here to recuperate."

Elly smiled at him, wishing just one thing had stayed un-normal: the locket. But the locket was only a pretty piece of jewelry now.

"No more nightmares, Elly?" Grandma asked. "No more fears?"

Startled, Elly considered this. She'd slept through several nights without one bad dream. "That's right," she said. And she'd played in the ravine and worked on the tree fort without one moment of fear. When had it all changed?

Then she knew. The nightmares had vanished the night she cut down the rope swing.

So had her fear of heights.

And so had the magic of the locket.

Suddenly, she understood. The locket had stopped

working the instant it was no longer needed—when Winnie was safe and Elly had conquered her fear.

"Gee Gee had a good day today," Grandma was saying. "Maybe you can come with me tomorrow, Elly, when I visit."

Elly nodded, smiling at the thought of seeing Winnie again, even as an old lady. "Did Gee Gee have a nickname when she was a girl?" she asked, wondering why she'd never heard of Gee Gee's being called Winnie. She might have figured things out weeks sooner if she'd only known.

Grandma shook her head. "She was just 'Eleanor,' like me. Although . . ." She paused for a minute. "I believe when she was young, one of her brothers pronounced 'l's' as 'w's' and she was called 'Winnie' for a time."

"Winnie?" Grandpa said. "I like that."

"Yes." Elly smiled to herself. "So do I."

As soon as they walked into Gee Gee's room, Elly could tell that she was still not herself.

"Elly!" Gee Gee cried gladly, but she didn't recognize Grandma. "Who's the old lady?" she whispered to Elly as she had done that other time.

They didn't stay long. Grandma tried to talk with Gee Gee, but she kept pulling away, like a little child. She was nothing like the woman Elly had known all her life—and nothing like Winnie.

As they were leaving, Elly paused at the doorway behind Grandma and looked back at Gee Gee. She was sitting in a chair by the window, a blanket covering her knees, her face lined and old. "Good-bye, Gee Gee," she said.

" 'Bye, 'bye," Gee Gee said like a little girl, her dimples flashing.

Winnie had had dimples.

A wave of love washed over Elly, and she flew back across the room. "Winnie," she whispered. She knelt and put her arms around the old, wrinkled woman.

"Elly?" Something in Gee Gee's voice made Elly pull back and look into her eyes.

Gee Gee squinted at her, as if she were struggling to remember something. "Elly . . ." she said again, frowning. "Elly . . ." Then suddenly she was again the familiar old Gee Gee. But she still looked puzzled. "*Was* it you? But how could it have been?"

"It was me," Elly whispered.

"I thought I'd dreamed that time in the ravine," Gee Gee said slowly. "I had been so lonely that summer . . ."

Elly nodded. Winnie's friend Helen had died, and Olivia had been seriously ill. "I found the locket in the Eleanor desk," she said.

"My Aunt Nellie gave it to me for my birthday," Gee Gee said. "And I remembered what you said. I always kept it in the secret place. But you never came back." She glanced away, as if remembering. "And then I grew up and forgot all about that time."

Her gaze came back to Elly, and her dimples appeared again. "Until you were born, and your mother called you 'Elly,' and then I did wonder—"

"Elly, dear." Grandma was at the door. "Mama. Is everything all right?"

Elly smiled into Gee Gee's eyes, Winnie's eyes. "Everything is fine, Grandma."

Then Gee Gee spoke. "I want you to give that box to Elly now, Eleanor."

The box was the size of a small book. A piece of paper had been taped to the top, which said, in Gee Gee's handwriting, "To be given to Elly the year she is eleven—after July twenty-eighth."

July 28. Shivers ran down Elly's spine.

Inside the box was one of Gee Gee's china angels, the one swinging on a swing.

It wasn't a rope swing. It was a regular kind of swing attached to poles, not to a tree, with a seat to sit on, not a big knot. But it was a swing, and the angel was smiling fearlessly as the swing lifted her above the tiny china circle of grass.

"I don't know why she wanted you to have that particular one," Grandma was saying.

Elly knew, but all she said was "Thanks, Grandma." She took the angel into her room and set it on top of the desk. Then she pulled out the little drawer in the middle and took off the locket.

She rubbed the tiny heart once more and then put it in the secret place. She didn't need its magic anymore. Maybe the locket worked only when an Eleanor needed magic. She had been terrified by nightmares and high places; Winnie had been lonely.

She replaced the little drawer, sliding it carefully over the locket. She and Winnie had both been Eleanors in need of magic. Had there been others? Grandma? Mom?

Elly put back the slant top of the Eleanor Desk, wondering if she'd ever know. For now, the locket would stay safe in its hiding place. Maybe no one would need its magic for years. Maybe not until the next Eleanor.

She smiled. She had often thought about what nickname she would give her daughter if she had one, and now she knew. The next Eleanor would be called Winnie.

MAKE TODAY YOUR ~~UN~~LUCKY DAY!
READ ALL 13
SPINETINGLERS BY
M. T. COFFIN

#1 The Substitute Creature   77829-7/$3.50US/$4.50Can

#2 Billy Baker's Dog Won't Stay Buried
77742-8/$3.50US/$4.50Can

#3 My Teacher's a Bug   77785-1/$3.50US/$4.50Can

#4 Where Have All the Parents Gone?
78117-4/$3.50US/$4.50Can

#5 Check It Out—and Die!   78116-6/$3.50US/$4.50Can

#6 Simon Says, "Croak!"   78232-4/$3.50US/$4.50Can

#7 Snow Day   78157-3/$3.50US/$4.50Can

#8 Don't Go to the Principal's Office
78313-4/$3.50US/$4.99Can

#9 Step on a Crack   78432-7/$3.50US/$4.99Can

#10 The Dead Kid Did It   78314-2/$3.50US/$4.99Can

#11 Fly by Night   78366-5/$3.50US/$4.99Can

#12 Killer Computer   78312-6/$3.50US/$4.99Can

#13 Pet Store   78460-2/$3.50US/$4.99Can

Buy these books at your local bookstore or use this coupon for ordering:

Mail to: Avon Books, Dept BP, Box 767, Rte 2, Dresden, TN 38225   E
Please send me the book(s) I have checked above.
❑ My check or money order—no cash or CODs please—for $_____ is enclosed (please add $1.50 per order to cover postage and handling—Canadian residents add 7% GST).
❑ Charge my VISA/MC Acct#_____ Exp Date_____
Minimum credit card order is two books or $7.50 (please add postage and handling charge of $1.50 per order—Canadian residents add 7% GST). For faster service, call 1-800-762-0779. Residents of Tennessee, please call 1-800-633-1607. Prices and numbers are subject to change without notice. Please allow six to eight weeks for delivery.

Name_____
Address_____
City_____State/Zip_____
Telephone No._____   MTT 0996